WE ARE NOT ALONE

John E. Parnell
and
Thomas E. Savage

"It seems that rarely does a day go by when evidence of aliens isn't reported somewhere in the world … Why?"

ISBN 978-1625122438

TABLE OF CONTENTS

CHAPTER ONE
Hiding in the Dark

A myriad of voices talked to each other over several channels, going through checks numbered in the hundreds. The rocket was a complex bomb that carried passengers and no one was leaving anything to chance. For Angela McGee, this was both the culmination of a dream and the next stage of a journey she had worked so hard to complete. She was already a graduate of the MIT master mathematics program and a decorated F-22 pilot in the air force. She was not just a soldier but a dedicated scientist ... exactly the kind of person NASA wanted in an astronaut. For her first mission, she was the co-pilot, ready to go and prove herself for future missions to come. She was not the kind of person that would ever stop dreaming and this would only be her first trip to space and the International Space Station.

Angela went through the on-board checks with captain Aaron Duffy. He was a mentor of sorts, a decorated astronaut that had already taken the trip several times. The others simply called him Duff as he was usually no nonsense and a man of few words. Next to the pair was the Russian cosmonaut Yuri Barikoff. The jovial Russian proved a fan of bad jokes and was affectionately nicknamed Cmex ... the Russian word for laughter. It somehow devolved into "Smeks." Angela had not yet earned her astronaut nickname but she hoped that after she proved herself in this mission she would get one. She was task focused and knew that she had a lot to offer both astronauts she was going up with even though they were veterans of the ISS.

Angela finished her checks and double checks, admitting that the space suit grew heavier the longer you wore it in earths gravity. She had trained heavily for this and her body was in peak physical condition. She had trained for months for what was to come next but Duff and Smeks both told her that nothing can truly prepare you for the G forces of liftoff. As the checks were completed Angela braced herself, she fought to temper her excitement lest it lead her to distraction. Though at this point there was little for her to do, she still needed to remain focused and alert to possible issues and be ready for anything. One of her courses in training for this mission was about observation and cataloguing facts. Even trained scientists have trouble reconciling the experience of space travel their first time. The human mind and body makes certain assumptions and they have to be focused and controlled to allow anything learned in space not to be biased. An astronaut was a scientist like no other. Angela recalled stories of early moon mission astronauts having to learn extreme geology to face a landscape they could not even begin to prepare for.

Angela focused her mind back on the present and away from her memories. As the countdown hit zero her heart skipped a beat. For a brief second, there was nothing, no noise, no talking. Then there was the boom. A massive explosion of highly complex fuel and boosters, followed by a titanic lurch of force. Angela could feel herself pushed into her chair like a pneumatic vice pressed against every inch of her body. Her subconscious told her that things were very wrong but her mind knew otherwise. The feeling was exhilarating and she could not help but smile as she pushed though it and the rocket began to streak toward the sky.

Duff of course said nothing ... lost in a superhuman like concentration that would not break unless he was needed to perform a task. Smeks was humming to himself, seeming to like the unique feeling of pressure and excitement. The forces continued and Angela had to focus to breath. Were she not prepared physically and mentally it might have been easy for the savage unforgiving force to knock the wind out of her and make normal breathing prohibitive. However, her stomach muscles were stronger that most women her age and she easily compensated. Even before the G forces started to burn off she started getting used to it.

"How are you feeling newbie?" Smeks asked with his usual jovial tone.

"Like I'm being hugged by gravity," Angela managed, trying to keep her voice as confident as possible despite the added exertion.

"Good," Smeks responded. "Because we would hate to have to pull over."

For several more moments that felt much longer, the force of multiple times earth pull pushed down on Angela. However, as the rocket broke free of the atmosphere it began to feel like reaching the top of a hill on roller-coaster. It was the feeling of gravity temporarily going from a push to a pull as inertia took over. However, unlike the roller-coaster, the downward pull did not reassert itself. It was like she kept going up forever. She had spent many flights on the "Vomit comet," the modified jet that dove at just the right angles to simulate weightlessness. However, now that she was truly feeling it, the sensation was night and day in difference. The feeling of going from oppressive gravity to none was intoxicating, like climbing out of a cold pool into a hot tub.

Angela gathered her concentration back to the moment. She was not on a pleasure cruise and had work to do. She went over a series of checks and procedures and parts of the rocket were ejected back to earth. Now free of the access baggage the capsule could begin its approach to the ISS. As Angela did her double-checks, a strange light streaked across her visor. She turned her head and shoulders to look out the small side window of the capsule. She saw a shape and colors she could not reconcile.

"Are you guys seeing this?" Angela asked, not sure what to think.

"It's beautiful!" Smeks replied. "Everyone gets all choked up when they first see the earth from space."

Angela realized that neither Duff or Smeks were even looking, writing off her curiously as her being a newbie. She did a couple more checks but was drawn to the strange sight again as the light changed colour. At first it was a pale blue but now a bright violet. She focused on the object, wondering if it might be a trick of the lights or a satellite of some kind. However, as she watched it the lights seemed to swirl around itself akin to a ring of light around a bright central sphere. It was moving in a way far to advanced to be used in space. All satellites and spacecraft were built for function over form. Sturdy white and grey tubes and boxes built for a harsh environment. However, this thing ... whatever it seemed to be, was beautiful. As fast as it had arrived it suddenly disappeared. The lights seeming to fold in on itself and streak outward, obscured by the shadows of deep space behind it. Angela shook off what she had just seen. She had work to do and the last thing she needed was to be distracted by a ghost in space.

***

The docking to the ISS was something that Angela had done in simulators close to four thousand times. Though it was a simple idea to line up the capsule and dock, even the smallest mistake could mean disaster, not just for the capsule but for all souls aboard the ISS. Duff told Angela to take command of the approach and docking, evaluating and waiting at the ready to assist if need be. Angela went to work, she knew every part of the procedure backwards and forwards and the calculations to the approach was something she could easily do in her head. Though she spoke four languages none were as fluent to her as math. It is said that mathematicians dream in equations and this was something Angela had long learned was not a joke. She focused her tasks and mind, and within a matter of minutes the capsule connected with the ISS connectors. The systems began to pressurize the capsule to the station.

"I think I forgot my toothbrush," Smeks said in mock urgency as he undid his safety restrains. "Mind if we swing by the store and pick one up."

"You can use a socket wrench for all I care," Duff replied as he undid his restraints. "This is home for me and were not going anywhere."

Angela undid her safety harness and was greeted by more anti gravity. She resisted the urge to play around, the feeling so delightful and freeing. She instead went to her task, gathering what needed and heading to the ISS.

After taking care of the setup and restocking, Angela could take a moment to relax. She was monitoring the com system as she looked out the round window to earth. The view as Smeks had said was spectacular, and she almost could not believe her eyes. Occasionally she would get a patch request from the panel and switch to different channels to compensate.

The previous team of astronauts look tired and ready to head back to earth. Their mission had been extended due to poor weather conditions delaying the launch of Angela and the others to replace them. As Angela worked with the communications controls a very grumpy Scotsman resided in a chair on the wall behind her, secured with a strap.

"You looking forward to going home?" Angela asked as she went over a procedure on a clipboard.

"I look forward to some real food," the Scott replied. "Something that won't float when you eat it or come from a pouch."

"I quite like astronaut rations," Angela joked. "I ate them as much as I could in training to get a taste for them."

"They ain't got no taste," The Scott joked. "I want some meat ... some potatoes ... some home cooked shepherds pie!"

"I've never had shepherds pie," Angela admitted. "My grandfather always went on about it though."

"What you doing up here then?" the Scott asked in mock offence. "You haven't experienced the best of earth yet you're not ready for the stars."

"We'll see," Angela said in an amused tone as she flipped through the audio channels, a strange pulsating tone flared up suddenly. "Hey what is this?"

"Oh, that is a glitch," the Scott said with a sigh. "Just ignore it."

"It almost doesn't sound random," Angela said as she focused on the tones for a moment.

"Let me fix that," the Scott sad as he undid his harness and floated over. He cut the power to the terminal then switched it back on. The tone was gone and the channel was clear. "There ye go. All fixed."

"Thanks," Angela said in a neutral tone ... wondering if that tone had been something worth investigating further. "Almost sounded like some kind of signal."

"Naw," the Scott responded. "Just your ears playing tricks on you."

Eventually the previous team had departed and Angela's team took over. The station could hold a larger crew but this mission did not require it. There was no big maintenance to be done and the experiments that needed to be performed did not require more hands. Angela could not get the strange occurrences out of her mind. The strange thing she had seen when she came up and the seemingly patterned tones. She spent as much time as she could spare looking out the windows and whenever she flipped through the audio channels she would hope for the tones to return. However, as the days went on she found less and less time to look for the unknown. There were always chores to be done and several of the experiments proved more troublesome than had been anticipated. As wondrous as space was she was looking forward to going home and taking some much-deserved time off. However, when the day to head home finally came she felt like she would do anything to stay. It was like a mortal finding their way to Mount Olympus and being told they had to climb back down. As her capsule left the station on it's careful journey back down to Terra Firma, Angela glanced back to the space station to say goodbye. She could swear she saw the strange glow once more but she had no way to tell for sure or time to double check.

***

After the fact, the mission seemed to go by in a blur. The time spent, the things learned, it all seemed like some fantastical dream. Angela had mentioned as much frequently during the trip and earned the nickname dreamer. She might have preferred a more proactive name, like her air force call sign "Solitaire," but she had made one of her dreams come true so who was she to argue.

Back on the ground there was extensive debriefing, long weight training to get over the prolonged weightlessness on the body and logging the results of the experiments. There was a lot more to being an astronaut then actually flying on rockets and she was part of all of it. She did press interviews, travelled to colleges and recruiting grounds but she found her most fulfilling endeavour was a trip to a second-grade classroom in her home town. She talked about how she became an astronaut, her training and what it was like to go to space. However, it was a simple question, straight from the innocent mind of a child that threw her off.

"Did you see any UFOs?" the young boy asked in a serious tone.

Angela had pushed the things she had seen and heard to the back of her mind. She had so much success on her mission and didn't want to taint it with recollections of strange sightings. Angela thought for a second on the best way to answer the question and not disappoint the child.

"There is a lot of cool stuff in space that you aren't always prepared for," Angela explained. "For example, you never know which way is up. You can look down at earth and feel like it is so far below, but it doesn't feel like it is down."

The children seemed to be interested in her stories and no further questions about UFOs and aliens were asked again.

As much as she tried to put what she had seen behind her, the events tugged at her mind. She could not help but think of Richard Dryfuss from *Close Encounters of the Third Kind* becoming obsessed with images he could not figure out. Angela did not fully believe what she had seen was alien or beyond explanation but she felt that she needed to express what she had seen ... or at least thought she had seen. She had a sketchbook that she liked to use to draw some of her ideas. She fancied herself as an artist in her youth and even though she didn't have as much time for it as she would like anymore she still liked to sketch. She roughed out the colours and the shapes, shading in the dark background of space to give it the contrast she remembered. She had no way of knowing if it was accurate to whatever it was but the sketch elicited the dame feeling when she looked at it.

As cathartic as drawing it was, she did not feel like she actually expressed what she had experienced. The doubt in her mind that it was some sort of optical illusion kept her from fully admitting what she saw was anything worth donating thought to. However, the math was something she could not deny. She took up her pencil again and on a fresh page begun to express what she remembered of the tones. She thought of it like mores code or binary, expressing the tones as lines or dots. Though she had not heard much of the tones she had an idyllic memory and remembered exactly what she had heard. As she finished the lines and dots she stared at it. She did not see anything at first but did not stop looking.

"OK ..." Angela said as she looked at the dashes. "This is nothing yet but there is a pattern in there somewhere."

Angela decided that she very likely did not get the entire message or code. So, she started to add bits to it at the beginning and end as if it were cut off. She tried a couple of options but before long realized by adding very little it became something that made sense. It seemed to be indicating a passage of time ... possibly a matter of minutes.

"Was someone trying to communicate a time interval?" Angela asked herself as she stared at the page in front of her. Her thoughts however were interrupted as her phone went off ... it was her commander at NASA.

The news that Angela was waiting for had finally come, there was another mission and NASA was very intent that she be on it. Though it had not been too long since her last mission, Angela could not wait to get up again. Not only was this the career she was passionate about, part of her brain knew that if there were answers about what she saw ... they would be up there.

A few months later Angela was back in a capsule and blasting off back to the space station. With her again were Duff and Smeks, but this time she could take the controls as the main pilot. She had impressed system control before with her accuracy and instincts and was thankful for a chance to shine. The liftoff happened without incident and Angela made her last checks before ejecting the booster. As weightlessness took over and the atmosphere faded to reveal the dark of space, Angela could not help but feel something akin to returning home.

As Angela began the approach to the ISS she saw something she could not reconcile. Dead ahead was the strange occurrence she had seen last time. It was larger and closer this time, the bright sphere orbited by the ring of bright lights. Angela considered getting the others attention but knew they both were doing their own procedures and she could not afford the distraction at this pivotal moment. She had to check and double check her approach telemetry and make sure the retro boosters fired to slow down the capsule. All she could do was devote a certain amount of her conscious mind to studying the phenomenon as best she could. She continued her work and it occurred to her there were indeed cameras on the front of the capsule. They weren't currently aiming where they needed to but she hoped as she got closer she could get the item on them. However, as she got closer and began to slow down she saw the strange object slowly move so the station was between itself and the capsule.

"It's hiding," Angela thought to herself, swearing it moved in response to the capsules approach and that showed signs of deliberate action ... and that meant intelligence.

As Angela made the final approach she did not see the object again. She completed the sequence and once again docked with the space station. She saw no more sign of anything out of the ordinary but having even seen it again meant to her that there was something out there. She decided that this was worthy of investigating further ... but she had to be careful. There was a two day overlap before the previous crew left and she decided that she had some questions for them.

The first person she had a chance to talk to was a Japanese astronaut named Hiro. She caught up with him in the hydroponics area as he was preparing to bring home his samples.

"Excuse me Hiro, might I have a moment of your time?"

"Of course," Hiro responded, floating on the wall with one hand bracing the wall and the other hand closing off a section of his project. "How can I be of service?"

"I was wondering if you have had any strange phenomenon," Angela asked, careful not to sound like she was straight up asking for UFOs.

"I tend not to see the forest from the trees," Hiro admitted. "Which is ironic as I am a botanist. Why though do you ask?"

"Silly reason really," Angela replied, deciding to write off her inquiry to Hiro as a joke. "Some kids at a school asked me what strange things I've seen so I am asking around."

"I swore I saw another vessel once," Hiro responded.

"Another vessel?" Angela asked in an encouraged tone. "What kind of vessel?"

"It was just space junk," Hiro said with a smile. "Just some old ESPN satellite that had a deteriorating orbit. Your eyes can play tricks on you up here."

Angela thanked Hiro and went in search of her next subject. A Canadian astronaut named Merrik. Merrik was an engineer and was just finishing up a video call home.

"Hey Merrik, you ever see any strange light phenomenon up here?" Angela asked. "I was having some issues with some pictures I took last time."

"Not really," Merrik replied. "I have had issues with lens flare but I have an anti-polarization lens now. Cleared it right up."

"Would be great to get some photos of some once on a lifetime stuff," Angela replied.

"Everything up here is once and a lifetime," Merrik replied. "Though most photos are the same ... blue on black all day long. Your eyes can play some tricks on you up here but the camera never catches anything."

"I guess you're right," Angela replied, realizing she would get no more from him.

Her last stop was an American pilot named Samson. He was the main pilot that brought the previous team up and the most likely to have seen what she saw.

"I had some issues on approach," Angela admitted. "I wonder if I could pick your brain."

"Of course," Samson replied as he looked over a list on a clipboard. "Was it mechanical?"

"Nothing like that," Angela replied. "I had some issues with the approach. I think something beyond the station was messing with my line of sight."

Samson turned to her and looked her in the eye. "There is nothing but deep space beyond the station ... don't let your eyes play tricks on you."

With that Samson headed off, unwilling to continue the conversation further.

Angela was left more confused then before. Though each of the other crew had offered little they all used the same phrase about eyes playing tricks. Angela could not help but think they were indeed hiding something and all seemed to have coordinated their response. Angela decided that there was nothing to be accomplished by pressing them and went back to work.

***

Angela's mission had become very busy and the ideas of strange phenomenon fell to the wayside to get it done. She did not ask any questions and did not see anything else. It wasn't until she returned home that her mind was brought back to it again. She was in a hotel room, preparing for an interview when she happened across something on the internet. It was an illustration, and though rudimentary it accurately showed what she had seen. She spent hours trying to track down the source but it was too well hidden. From the angle, she decided it had to be another astronaut but she had no way of knowing who or even when it was drawn.

By the time of her third mission she had a bad feeling on her mind. There was defiantly something up there, she had seen it, someone else had too and there were people guarding their words about it. She kept her eyes open on the third trip but did not see any sign of the strange phenomenon. However, as she approached the ISS for the third time she could almost FEEL like there was something behind the station, just out of sight and in hiding in the dark shadows of space.

The previous crew was to leave the same day and it was the same crew she had relieved last time. They seemed busy, annoyed, and seemed unwilling to talk with her this time. Angela focused on keeping to her work, she was in space to be a scientist, not to be a detective.

Two days later Angel was using the coms, doing maintenance and checking off from a long checklist. However, as she turned the dial a familiar sound came on ... the strange pulsing. Angela stopped what she was doing, taking out a pen and started to log the dashes on a fresh piece of paper. She could hang onto the signal for close to ten minutes before it went silent. She folded up the paper and put it in her pocket to focus on finishing her official work. However, the idea of going over it would not leave her mind.

Later that day she had some free time and took out the paper. She went over the numbers, trying to find a pattern. Now having more of the sequence, it made more sense, evolving into a countdown of sorts and ending with a series of coordinates. She was not sure where the coordinates were but as she cross referenced they seemed to indicate off the eastern seaboard of the United States. This had been some manner of communication basically stating, "In a short time ... go down."

Angela could not reconcile what she had just figured out and checked it four more times to confirm it was correct. The signal was radio so that meant that it was from the vicinity around the ship ... coming from space. It was not the binary signal of a satellite and was nothing of terrestrial origin. Also, the space above earth was tightly regulated with only a handful of people and any return to earth was something of great fanfare. There was something else up here and it was going down to earth soon.

Angela determined as best she could when the time was that it was supposed to happen and turned on a camcorder. She filmed out a window, admitting to herself that she did not know what she expected to see. However, as the time came there was nothing out the window. Just as Angela thought that she was wasting her time the outer walls of the ISS began to shake. It was low at first but grew louder and more intense before abruptly stopping.

"What was that?" Angel said out loud. "Did something just pass us?"

Angela took the camcorder to Duff and showed him the footage. Though there was nothing visible, the sound was loud enough to make the lens of the camera shake.

"What do you think?" Angela asked. "I'm surprised you didn't feel it yourself."

"It's nothing," Duff said as he took the memory card out of the camcorder and put it in his pocket. "Your ears were just playing tricks on you."

Angela smiled and agreed though she knew deep down she was being lied to. She had heard and felt something and there were people trying to cover it up. She knew that if she pushed the issue she might be grounded from further missions, so she decided to eagerly play along as if to avoid suspicion.

Duff kept Angela busy for the rest of the trip, seemingly convinced she believed him there was nothing, however deciding he would not let her have any more opportunity to experience anything out of the ordinary. Upon return to earth she was visited by a NASA psychiatrist named Dr. Guis. Angela was used to talking to such people as astronauts were under intense mental scrutiny, but rarely did they come after a mission. She suspected Duff mentioned the recording and this was a result.

"How are you finding the missions?" Guis asked. "You have had a few back to back."

"I love it," Angela responded, careful not to give up any indication that she thought the interview was strange.

"Good, good," Guis responded. "You have been under considerable stress and I wonder if you might have had any issues ... seen anything."

"Oh, just the usual hard work and lack of sleep," Angela said with a smile. "You know the thing ... be observant, but everything is usually just ice or echoes."

"You didn't see anything that gave you reason to pause?" Guis asked in a serious tone.

"Of course not," Angela replied. "There nothing up there but space and more space. Anything else is just your eyes playing tricks on you."

Guis smiled, seeming to have bought her deception. She was given a green light and everyone hinted there would be another mission for her soon enough. Angela however felt worse, there definitely was something up there and people knew about it. Something was being covered up and she narrowly lost her job for them to do it.

Two weeks later she was attending a conference in Prague when there was a knock at her door. Angela was not expecting visitors and slowly opened it. It was Smeks, who entered the room without invitation and closed the door behind him.

"You saw it, right?" Smeks asked in a cautious tone. "Heard it?"

"I don't know what you are talking about," Angela stated. "Are you alright Smeks?"

"You don't have to lie to me," Smeks insisted. "Don't tell me anything about my eyes playing tricks! I know you saw it your first mission. It shook the station last time."

"I didn't know what you saw experienced it too," Angela admitted. "You seemed so closed off about such things."

"That is what you do when they are watching," Smeks replied. "I drew it ... I put it on the net and others confirmed they have seen it too. Others that have been to the ISS."

"I saw your drawing," Angela commented. "I made one just like it."

"There is something up there," Smeks replied. "They are hiding near the ISS."

"I think they are doing it to piggyback on our signals," Angela responded. "They can hide behind us and cover their actions with ours. The ISS blasts loudly on almost every frequency there is ... that's a lot of noise to be lost in."

"What are they doing?" Smeks asked. "For what reason?"

"I don't know," Angela admitted. "But they are sending things down to earth."

Smeks sighed. "This is really troubling and I don't know who we can go to about this."

Angela nodded. "I agree. That recording almost got me grounded."

"Say nothing," Smeks admitted. "Though there is something up there, NASA is the one that controls the secrets. This conversation never took place."

Without any more words Smeks left and closed the door behind him. Angela sat down and looked out the window to see the night sky. She had more questions than answers but knew that it would be very dangerous if she asked them.

For now, all she could do is sit in silence and wonder what was hidden in the dark above.

CHAPTER TWO
The Place in the Universe

Angela still had a bad taste in her mouth over the entire situation. She no longer had the benefit of doubting that what she saw was real or that there was no cover up. There was too much evidence and other people who had experienced what she had experienced to ignore. However, knowledge of being right offered no solace and this added to her frustration. She was on a lull in her work and responsibilities. There was another mission up at the ISS and there were currently no booked appearances or events. Angela was confident that NASA still thought she was in good standing so it was only a matter of time until she got another mission. So, in the mean time all she could do is find some way to express herself and work through the energy of not being able to do anything about what she saw. She found herself in the gym, though she was not training for a mission she always liked to keep in peak physical form. She started with intense cardio, switched to weights, and ended up punching and kicking a heavy bag. She was not used to having so much anger, so much pent up emotion she could not deal with and this was the only thing she could do about it. She pushed herself further and further even the most fervent of gym goers stopped to watch the woman with a plan attack her workout. By the end, when her body finally had enough and her mind was exhausted enough to relax she walked from the gym, caked in sweat and ready to think on what to do next.

As much as she knew that she should give up she knew that she could not. Angela had always been the type of person that when faced with a task or challenge, would stop at nothing to overcome it. She had no basis for how one could just drop something, especially something so monumental as the secret in space. The choice was simple ... would it be easier to force herself to forget what she saw and experienced or would it be harder to keep fighting for the truth. As much as the idea of becoming permanently grounded was, the idea that she would have to live on for a lie forever with no attempt for truth was even harder. She knew herself well enough to know that she could not just drop it but if she were to keep searching she had to be smart about it. If she was against a system of secrets and ever watching eyes she had to do her searching silently and create the ruse that she was still an obedient rook that never questioned what was told to her. By the time Angela got home, she was physically exhausted. However now that she had made the decision that she would not give up on her personal mission for the truth she was more emotionally relaxed. As she went to sleep, the idea that she would begin the next phase of her investigation in the morning finally allowed her the solace she so needed.

The original searches on the internet Angela had done were both foolish and sloppy. Luckily, she had not uncovered much of real importance but if she had it might have caused trouble if NASA was watching. She had a few connections from her university days and called in a few favours. What she got was a laptop that was difficult to trace and if she used public internet there would be no trace of her name upon her searches. She began a series of clandestine searches, each one at a different coffee-shop with free WiFi. She had no real way to know where she should even start looking but knew that the only way to find something was to start. The main issue with the searching was getting past the seemingly unending amount of fluff and fake reports. There were a lot of people who wanted the attention of reporting fake sightings of extra terrestrials and even if they were like what she was looking for there was no way to see if they were genuine. However, despite the search engine, despite the search parameters it seemed that the tripe was what came up first every time. She leaned back and sighed, raising her arms over her head.

"Search engines aren't unbiased," a voice said from next to her.

"Excuse me?" Angela said, looking to her screen then to person who interjected. It was a teenage boy with tan skin and dark hair. He was dressed in a t-shirt and baggy pants and had a large laptop with a page full of code.

"You're searching for something," the young man replied. "Search engines are actually designed to give you specific types of results."

"What do you mean?" Angela replied, seemingly convinced that the teen could not see what she was looking for, instead focusing on the nature of her frustration. "Isn't google the best way to search for something?"

"It both is and isn't," the boy replied. "If you are asking it for something simple and common like a recipe for cake and it will give it to you. However, if you want the recipe to a less common kind, you must sift through the more popular options."

"I'm getting a lot of that," Angela admitted. "A lot of parodies and click-bait mostly."

"Google and search engines of the kind prioritize popular results," the boy explained. "It is like looking for a restaurant ... people usually want to know the best ones and it priorities those."

"Why does it do that?" Angela asked. "What if you are looking for a less common result?"

"Time mostly," the boy replied. "The pure number of pages and sites on the internet is a nearly infinite number over billions of servers. To truly search everything would take longer than most people would have the patience to wait for. Early on in search engines they only looked for tags, like bookmarks so they didn't have to start from the bottom. However, google is so popular as it not only looks for the keywords they look for the interactions with the subjects. If you want cake it looks and sees ... hey this cake is the most popular, let us offer that first."

"What if I make the query more specific?" Angela asked, looking back to her screen.

The boy nodded. "That is the easiest way. There are a lot of words and phrases that are very similar. Say you are searching for a way to get something unstuck from glue ... and the most popular similar response is the song stuck like glue. Your results will be lost unless you specify exactly what you want."

"I am trying that but it seems that no matter how I phrase it there is a ton of garbage that comes up," Angela admitted, staring at her computer screen with disgust.

"Well, there's a lot of crap out there," the boy continued. "It's like a radio wave. You got the signals you want in there but everyone is broadcasting as loud as they can to get your attention. Search engines can be influenced by things like click bait, advertisers, and governments."

"Governments?" Angela asked. "They can interfere with search results?"

"Of course they can!" the boy replied. "They have the motive, the resources, and most people wouldn't even suspect it. There is something you want hidden why not just hire analysts to flood the internet with red herrings so no one could tell the truth from the lies. The best part is its hard to find out who even did it."

"I think that is what is happening," Angela admitted. "Is there anything that can be done?"

"Have you tried the deep web?" the boy asked. "It is almost completely unregulated and not affected by common search engine algorithms."

"What is the deep web?" Angela asked. "How do I get to it?"

"It is also known as the invisible web," the boy began. "Think of the internet like an iceberg. Like I said, it is a massive chunk of information both used and discarded. The part that you use ... google, Netflix, Gmail ... that stuff is all at the top and fast and safe. However down, below the "water" is the unsorted mass of information. Kind of like a giant storage locker and the deeper you go the less organized or regulated the things are there. It is a place that is hard to police and people are more free with information there. Keep in mind this is a den of vipers. There is a lot of drugs, crime, and really terrifying pornography down there ... but they also have what you might be looking for ... a place where people are talking about whatever you are looking for free of prying eyes."

"How do I access this place?" Angela replied. "Can you help me?"

"Fifty bucks," the boy replied. "No names, no questions. I will hook you up and help you look."

"I'll give you a hundred," Angela replied. "So, you remember the extra money instead of what we find."

"Deal," the boy responded as he moved in closer and set up his laptop next to Angela. "You can refer to me as Octan."

"You can call me Solitaire," Angela replied, realizing she got to pick her pseudonym this time.

"Sounds good, Solitaire," Octan replied as he began to install programs to access the deep web onto Angela's computer. "What are we looking for?"

"Aliens," Angela admitted.

"Outstanding," Octan replied. "But you might have to be more specific."

Angela paused, wondering how much she should tell the boy. However, going over the moves she has made the last few days the odds that this boy could have positioned himself as a spy was mathematically improbable. She would watch her words but give him what she got.

"There are reports of strange sightings by the international space station. Strange craft that shift shape and a radio signal that is using complex mathematical structures to co-ordinate with other areas on earth."

"That I can work with," Octan replied as she began to search through message boards on the deep web. Angela was impressed. Different from the bright and polished sites of the regular net, the deep web was much more basic. There were no bells and whistles and everything was far more utilitarian."

"So, do you make some sort of algorithm?" Angela asked. "Like some sort of hacker program to search out the results?"

"No, that's bullshit," Octan replied. "Hacking as it's usually portrayed as a visual representation of something far more boring. Hacking is coding and reading and it takes much longer. What most people think is that hacking is just windows opening and closing and techno wizards making the plot move with digital dues ex-machina."

"Then what are we going to do?" Angela asked, realizing her whole idea of hacking was based on movies."

"We do this the old-fashioned way," Octan replied. "We look. We both go from alien message board to message board and look for anything that looks like what you are describing. Between the two of us we can get a lot done."

"Sounds good," Angela replied, taking to her laptop and watching Octan go to on his own. She took to it like any challenge and that was one challenge at a time, scanning online documents for the key phrases she was looking for. "I am shocked by the pure number of conspiracies I am seeing here."

"No doubt," Octan replied. "A lot of people in power have been covering up a lot of shit. That leaves a lot pf people desperate for a sympathetic ear and to discover they are not alone."

"Oh, I know that feeling," Angela admitted. "All too well."

***

Over the next week, Angela continued to meet with Octan, moving from coffee shop to coffee shop to complete the defence against tracking. Though Octan was young, he seemed to get more and more invested in the conspiracy and seemed to legitimately want to help her. They devised a code on how to figure out where to meet and kept working. Though the deep web had proven to be a less bogged down area for censorship and chafe it was also where the conspiracy theorists went to town. It was not so much that they were lying for attention, it was that any little or hard to explain thing was thought of a big conspiracy and blown way out of proportion. Angela even amusingly found record that her latest re-entry in the capsule was thought to be part of some sort of cover-up. Though as time went on it began to occur to Angela that the information she was looking for might just not be there to be found.

"I worry ..." Angela said as she leaned back and yawned. "Even with NASA not censoring these results the information might not have just gotten to the right people."

"I was thinking about something similar," Octan admitted. "Perhaps we are looking in the wrong areas."

Angela raised an eyebrow, "How so?"

"Well, NASA controls most of the information about going into space," Octan replied. "Even with the Russians and Chinese going there, NASA pretty much has a hand in what is done and said. However, there are other people looking at space even if they don't go there."

"NASA has their hands in most telescopes," Angela added. "They control most things that have any kind of accuracy looking at space."

"Not everything!" Octan replied as he spun his laptop around for Angela to see. "A space monitoring array in south America has been monitoring low orbiting space. They are currently doing research in the trajectories of low hanging space debris that might cause a problem to future space missions as well as the environmental impacts."

"They aren't regulated by NASA?" Angela asked, looking over the information on the screen.

"They wanted to be involved with NASA," Octan continued. "It is an outdated installation and NASA seemed to not believe in any real benefit in sticking time or money into it. As far as NASA is concerned this place is beneath it's notice and does not exist."

Angela pondered for a moment. It had all the hallmarks of a place that might have information that NASA has not yet buried. She knew that it would not have been able to see anything, but if she could get a full or partially full record of the strange transmission that would arm her with the first hard proof of the search.

"I think it would be foolish to try and email them or call them. NASA may not care much about them but such a query might pique their interests."

"Agreed," Octan replied. "Too bad we can't just go down there."

"I actually can," Angela said with a smile. "In my line of work getting flights is kind of easy and cheap."

Octan smiled, "I would like to stay on the case if that is alright with you. I will keep working on looking for more leads for you and contact you along the way. I'll set up a secure line of communication so you can leave messages for me even if its on a public computer. Perhaps we could make a code."

"I would be honored for more help," Angela said with a smile. "I will need all the help I can get to get to the bottom of this."

Angela spent the next few days getting all the information she could about the South American radio array. She needed to know how to get to it and how it worked so she would not have to waste time when she got there. Though she was well versed on radio technology, the stuff she was going to see was at least thirty years old and she had to brush up.

Old radio manuals were not hard to find and would provide substantial reading for the long journey down. She left Octan with enough money to pay him for his time and if he needed any more equipment or resources. She admitted she was growing to enjoy the lads company and was thankful that he was staying on the search for truth.

Angela knew better than to think that her movements would not be monitored and did not want to waste how careful she had been to dodge suspicion. She knew if she flew right down to where the array was it would not take a genius at NASA to figure out that she was on her way to the array. Instead, she planned an elaborate vacation starting form further north and moving down to it through seemingly random travels. Given the stress and chaos of her recent life even the pretense of a vacation was probably a good idea. She would also use the time to document her trip for Facebook, greater adding to the illusion she had just chosen the area as an optimal vacation locale.

Every day on her trip she spent the day relaxing ... though deep down, her mind was all business. At night, she would link up with Octan and discuss any developments. They had not just found a way to disguise their correspondence but had come up with a code on how to talk. It was troublesome at first to use it, but day by day it started to become second nature. To anyone reading the conversations it would seem like boring talk of internet memes and funny videos, but hidden to any but them it was detailed discussions about reported sightings and NASA cover-ups. On the back of Angels Head always was the array, as she travelled from town to town, she grew ever closer and was always thinking about what answers it might have. Soon she was in a small city called Tulatu and it was just four miles of jungle between her and the array. She thought of taking the road but decided that it might be monitored. Though she found no evidence of NASA's presence, she could not allow herself to believe that they were letting such a place go unchecked. She found record of an old tourist trail and packed to hike it herself.

Though she was in peak physical shape, Angela was not prepared for just how hot South America was. The elevation of the forested mountains did nothing but make it harder to breathe and the miles took more out of her than she cared to admit. By the time she was half way there, she was caked in sweat and very glad she brought as much water as she did. She had read up on how to navigate the forest safely and kept vigilant. She did not want her trip cut short due to a misstep or mistake. Along the trip there was not another soul in sight. Angela was thankful for this, not just because of weariness of NASA eyes, but because this was a region writhe with bandits. She had heard tales the night before of a recent tour group that was taken for ransom and she did not want to get caught up in that.

Soon enough the forest opened up to reveal a football field sized area of brush that had been cleared for the array. It was something like a villain's hideout from a bond film, a giant circular dish cut onto the forest itself, lined with aging and rusted steel mesh. In the centre was a massive antenna tower and to the side the observatory that operated it. Angela slowly made her way around to the front. She considered what she would say to get in but found the door open with music playing inside. She carefully went in, looking around and taking the place in. There were a series of desks, all with piles of old paper with no apparent sign of order. Likely the only people who worked here on a consistent basis were students and they seemed to have disappeared once their research was done. She then became aware that there was an almost singing sound coming from deeper within, alerting her to a live presence in the facility.

She went deeper in to the main floor of the observatory, ancient computers hummed and reel to reel hard drives whirled in their own hypnotic pace. Newer laptops and routers were plugged in, linked to the ancient technology with a Frankenstein-like collection of plugs and wires. Sitting in a swivel chair near one of the control areas was a slim lanky man with long grey hair and a matching beard. He was scribbling notes in an old notebook with a headset to one ear. He had been singing but seemed to have stopped for a moment to write.

"Hello?" Angela said as she walked into the room. "Are you in charge around here?"

"Oh!" The man said as he swivelled in his chair. "Barbara so good to see you!"

"Barbara?" Angela asked in confusion. "I don't know who that is."

"Oh Barbara, so good to see you," the man replied. "I was worried that you finished your dissertation and went home already."

"No, I'm still here," Angela replied, realizing that this both offered her an alias and a potential in with the man. She read his name tag to learn his name was Will. "Anything new and exciting ... Will?"

"Oh, very much so!" Will responded. "Big things indeed. All manner of things have been happening ... both good and bad!"

"Why don't you tell me all about them?" Angela said as she started fiddling with a nearby decrepit coffee machine. "I will make us some coffee."

"Excellent," Will replied. "There are some strange things going on. I think we may have a conspiracy on our hands."

"We do?" Angela asked, encouraged by this development. "What kind of conspiracy?"

"Bees!" Will responded. "They are here to take the bees!"

Angela sighed, thinking that the man might in fact be completely mad. "Who is trying to take the bees?"

"Not sure yet," Will responded. "But I think it is aliens."

"Aliens are after Earths' bees?" Angela replied in a skeptical tone, starting to think that her whole trip had been a colossal waste.

"Yes, yes!" Will responded. "People are always talking about how aliens are abducting people. But people are probably the least interesting or useful beings on this planet. People are evolved into a rather small margin ... we eat sleep ... SCREW ... but ultimately, we are just apes. Bees ... BEES, on the other hand, are marvels of evolution and we only know a fraction of what they do. Bees have been disappearing for years. They say that it's pollution but I know better."

"Yeah must be bees," Angela replied as she gave Will a cup of over-filtered coffee. "I think I might have to go to town, I ..."

"The signal proves it," Will responded before taking a sip of his coffee.

"Signal?" Angela said, her interest re piqued.

"Yes, the strange signal," Will responded. "I thought it was garbage at first but as I recorded it. It seemed to have a pattern that was not random. It is some sort of coordinated beacon and I think it is so they can take the bees."

"OK forget the bees for a second," Angela pleaded. "Did you figure out what the signal is doing?"

Will shook his head. "I am no mathematician ... that was the Asian kid ... what was his name Chu?"

"I am good with numbers," Angela replied. "Could I look at what you have ... you said you recorded it?"

"Yes," Will replied, but suddenly looked sad. "Well I did. But those guys who were asking questions last week accidentally blanked the tapes."

Angela felt a sinking feeling. It had to be NASA realizing that someone else might have recorded the strange signal from space. She realized that she probably would have no way to prove it or study it, but at least she could now know that they at least had knowledge of the signal. "They blanked all of it? That's unfortunate. Can you get more?"

"We can," Will responded. "Though the signal is actually quite slow by the time we get it here. It will take months to record a complete cycle again."

"I guess that is a start," Angela said, not particularly wanting to spend months in the array.

"I could just go to the backups I suppose," Will responded. "But that is a pain in the ass if you ask me."

"Backups?" Angela asked in shock. "There are backups?"

"Of course, there are," Will responded. "This place has been backing up everything over radio to the recording site five miles to the south. Not many people go there but it records everything we get from the dish just in case. Getting a few interns next month and was going to have them go there and get it then."

Angela smiled and raised an eyebrow. "Can you show me how to get there on a map, Will? I think I might just go there right now."

***

Restocking water and some supplies, Angela headed out at once. She knew that even thought there was a backup that it might not remain a secret for very long. If NASA had gone to such great lengths to silence the original recordings they would be unlikely to not think of the idea there might be a backup occurred to them.

The jungle beyond the array was much thicker and decidedly more treacherous, the path leading from the facility was very overgrown and likely the job of one of the interns to clear. This was encouraging, because if someone else were to have been out there, they would have been more breaks in the dense foliage. Angela could take solace in the fact that no one had tread where she was going in some time. There will be all manner of bugs, snakes, and other dangerous creatures in this place and she could only imagine how so many college students lasted so long out here. She supposed that it was likely this place was thought to be an adventure and they had no way of knowing that it was as alien here as another world until they got here. Angela was no stranger to dealing with harsh environments, part of her early NASA training was survival and spent time in jungles and forests like this in various exercises. She knew how to move carefully, what not to touch, and what not to disturb.

As she walked by one of the areas she could hear chainsaws somewhere in the distance and the telltale sounds of heavy vehicles. It was not unheard of for companies and groups to claim an area and clear-cut it but the distance from a main road made this place more trouble than it was worse. If there were people fighting to clear this area it was likely to get somewhere and that meant one of two things. It was NASA heading for the backup area or it was a drug cartel. Angela found the idea of a drug cartel more promising and this fact surprised her. The drug cartel was not after what she was after and likely would not care about anything she did here as long as it did not interfere with their business.

Angela hastened her steps, she was not optimistic enough to believe that the sounds ahead were not heading for the backup station and she needed to get there first. She had the benefit of terrain. There was a swampy marshy area by a small river and she knew that the group clearing the way would have to navigate around it. Angela could feel her boots sinking into the earth as she walked, threatening to turn into quicksand lest she get too far from the more solid mud path. Visuals of people trapped in quicksand from movies and TV floated into her head.

She knew that usually such things were not as dangerous but in such a harsh environment, once you got past your knees you were unlikely to get out without help.

She knew that she had very little time as the small building came into view. The place was just a massive storehouse for the information, hooked up to powerful solar panels and protected from the elements. She arrived at the door and took out the keys that Will had given her. She hastily opened the door and stepped in. Sets of automated lights began to flicker on and off as the aging technology struggled to do what it was supposed to do. The servers seemed relatively new compared to the reel to reel system of the compound, likely a somewhat newer addition that bordered on proving more trouble then it was worth. There were banks and banks of servers from various generations of technology lining the walls. Luckily Angela had gotten some information from Will as where to start looking. Though the man was a bit of a hoarder he did keep detailed notes. Before long Angela located the bank and fired up a screen. She found what she was looking for very quickly, an archive of recordings of the alien signal, all organized by date and time. There was a lot of it, surely enough to get a real look at it and get a better idea of what it might be.

Angela took out a thumb drive and after several moments of jury rigging she could hook it to the server and start downloading the information. She found it funny how large a computer was used for this size of information when this was new and how small it could be stored on now. As the download chugged away, Angela took a step back and stretched her arms. The long travel and harsh climate was beginning to take its toll and she was growing quite fatigued. She looked forward to getting the information and fleeing back to her hotel and taking a well-deserved rest. However, her positive plans were interrupted as she heard a gun click behind her. She turned slowly to see a young woman, not much older than she, standing by the door with a gun.

"Turns out this place might have something valuable after all," the woman replied, wiping her black hair out of her face with her free hand. "I told them we should have checked this place out weeks ago."

"Who are you?" Angela asked defiantly. "Why are you covering things up?"

The woman laughed. "This is not a movie. I am not going to waste any time telling you anything. You answer MY questions or you get shot. Is that understood?"

"Understood," Angela replied defiantly.

"Good," the raven-haired woman replied, taking out a pair of handcuffs from her bag. She tossed them to Angela who instinctively caught them. "Cuff your arms up to that metal loop above you. Feed it through and make it tight. If I think that you can slip them, I might just shoot you instead."

Angela sighed, locking one of the cuffs around her wrist tightly before reaching up and feeding the other cuff through the loop. She then cuffed her other hand tightly and looked at the woman with a look of defiant disgust.

"OK, next question," the rave-haired woman responded with a satisfied nod. "I presume you are downloading a copy of the classified signal?"

"Yeah," Angela replied, realizing there was no point in lying. "It is the last full copy we might use to decipher it's meaning."

"That is of no concern of yours," the woman replied. "Tell me who you are?"

Angela felt relieved, the woman seemed not to specifically be after her and that was something. She took a deep breath. "Jessica Atreides. I am a reporter for the *Toronto Sun*."

The woman perked an eyebrow. "I am sure at least half of that is a lie but, ultimately, it doesn't matter. You need to understand the lengths that we go to, to keep things the way they ... should be. We took care of the interns that manned the facility and, were it not for the advantage of how crazy the guy running it was, we would have taken him out too."

"So, the secrets of the people you work for are worth lives then?" Angela asked, anger evident in her tone. "This is potentially the most miraculous discovery in the history of mankind and here you are killing people to hide it. What is the point?"

"Again, you seem to think I can be coaxed into telling you the big picture?" the woman replied. "Ultimately it does not matter who I am any more than it matters who you are. I'm going to take your thumb drive for proof and then I'm going to wipe this place. There are people who will find out how dangerous you are then you disappear ... easy as that."

"Well it seems you hold all the cards then," Angela said defiantly, looking up at her cuffed hands.

"Who needs cards when you hold the gun?" the woman asked, sitting down and relaxing for a moment as she checked in on the transfer. She then looked down to her boots which were muddy and soaked from an obvious run in with the river. "I look forward to leaving this place. It is easier for people to disappear here however ... I'll give it that."

Angela looked around and weighed her options. As she first tugged on the loop above her, she realized something the woman had not seen. Though it was a solid loop of metal, it was screwed into what looked like hardwood, but was instead only panel. With a hard yank the whole metal loop would come out of the wall and free her. She knew she had to use this to her advantage and timing would be her only hope. If she messed it up she would be at the woman's mercy and get shot for sure. The woman sighed, seeming to be annoyed in how long the transfer was taking. She removed her muddy boots and soaked socks and tried to do her best to dry them out. This would be an advantage if Angela could do what she was planning, because she knew the woman would not be as agile in bare feet in the rough terrain.

With a close eye on the progress bar Angela mentally prepared herself for what was about to happen. She was no stranger to danger and stress and knew all to well how to slow her heart rate and prepare to stay fluid during difficult things. Just as the progress bar filled and the transfer finished the woman turned her gaze from her footwear to the computer screen. Angela ripped the grommet free and swung her hands down, striking the woman with both palms, sending her back off her chair and onto the floor beyond. Angela had hoped she would have dropped the gun but it was too late. She pulled the thumb drive out of the computer, put it in a pocket and sprinted out the door. Even with her cuffed hands, Angela was fast on the terrain, making it several yards before she heard any sign of pursuit from the woman with the gun.

Angela soon realized she had greatly underestimated the woman and even barefoot after an attack, she could keep up with her. A shot was fired, splintering a tree next to Angela and stopping her in her tracks. Angela slowly turned but before she could even consider surrender the woman gasped and slid down an embankment to the side. Her feet plunged into pliable earth and sank to her calves. She fought to keep her gun on Angela as she tried to get out but all the mud did was suck the girl's legs deeper, climbing over her knees and locking her in.

"Get me out of here!" the woman demanded, waving her gun at Angela.

"I think you will find a gun can't get you out of quicksand," Angela said as she moved to put a tree between most of her body and the gun. "You are the one who needs to listen to me now."

"I could just shoot you!" the woman replied as the mud climbed up her thighs, causing her to grow rigid, trying to move as little of her body as she could. "I really want to."

"I will help you out of that quicksand," Angela replied. "But I want the gun and the key to my handcuffs."

"Oh, is that how it is?" the woman said, looking up at Angela with a defiant expression, the quicksand slowly claiming her waist. "I give away my leverage, let you go and then tell you everything. Is that how it is?"

"Pretty much," Angela admitted. "Though I am rather not fond of you and who you likely work for, I have no desire to see you die in quicksand. The crew you likely hired and your companions are a far way off still and you know how hard it is to get through the brush. I am your only hope."

"You clearly know little about who I work for," the woman said as she looked down at the quicksand hungrily consume her body. "I am much more afraid of defying them then I am of this quicksand."

"What do you mean?" Angela asked. "What could be worth this?"

"My only solace ..." the woman replied as she put the gun to her head. "Is that you will learn nothing from me."

"Wait no!" Angela shouted but the gunshot rang out before she could say more. Birds flew into the air from the sound but soon the massive jungle continued, obscuring the horrific act from the rest of the world. Angela could only stare in disbelief as the quicksand claimed what was left of the mysterious woman, leaving her alone to start the long trek back to civilization.

***

It was a long walk back to town to Angela's hotel, she was still handcuffed and the idea that she might be followed weighed heavily on her mind. By the time she was sure she had eluded surveillance and made it back to the hotel, it was dark and she was exhausted. She walked to the front desk and looked at the concierge.

"Are you alright miss?" the concierge asked. "Do you wish for me to call the police?"

"That will not be necessary," Angela said as she awkwardly pulled a fifty out of her pocket and slid it on the counter. "I am not looking to answer any questions but if you could send up your maintenance guy to my room with some tools that would be great."

The concierge nodded, and shortly after Angela returned to her room, the maintenance supervisor arrived with a drill. It was not long before the locks on her cuffs were drilled and she was free. She gave the maintenance guy a big tip that ensured his silence as well. Angela took a long shower and contemplated what had occurred. Though she had indeed found what she was looking for, the haunting final moments of her would-be captor would not leave her mind. The woman had made her choice but Angela could not help but feel responsible. She was a strong-willed woman and just had to find a way to analyze what had happened to make it make sense to her. It was not she that had done this. It was not her fault that there were people who would hurt and kill for secrets. She had only discovered things and the people who had proven that the information was of life or death, importance had done the rest. People had already died for these secrets and Angela should feel lucky that she was not one of them.

As Angela dressed in fresh clothes she went over her next moves. Luckily the woman had left Angela with a solid position. She had not made any calls nor dealt with the people she was with. There was no one that had Angela's name that could link her to the information. Even the reclusive professor was certain she was indeed a different person and would answer questions as such. This was her first big advantage ... she had a complete record of the signal and NASA had no way of knowing that she did. The crew cutting their way to the recording station would destroy everything there, fully thinking they had silenced it once and for all. The woman would likely never be found and all that she had known or seen would be lost with her.

Angela took a quick rest and moved on in the morning. To keep up the appearances on the trip she had to be to her next place without delay. She had paid for extra nights in the hotels proceeding and after this stop so it would seem as if she bypassed it and could never be placed within twenty miles of the observatory. She arrived at the next hotel and kept up with the facade of her vacation. That evening she talked again to Octan, sending him a part of the recovered signal she had received.

Octan put it through a few descriptors and Angela went at it a bit with a notebook. However, the pure size of the recording and the not knowing where it started or ended provided a challenge. After a few tries both Angela and Octan had to admit they were in over their heads. Angela decided to sit on the information for awhile and finish her trip. Even though it was a sham, she decided she needed a few days to relax after what she had just been through.

Once she got back home she met up with Octan and was eager to get back to work on the recordings. She met up with her accomplice and friend at a coffee shop and took a seat in the back.

"How was your trip?" Octan asked, knowing full well most of what went on.

"Frankly, when you have been to space, South America pales in comparison," Angela said with a laugh.

Octan smiled and laughed, "Well, sure beats being here your whole life. Anyway, I have had little luck with the document. It is way over my head to get much out of it beyond seeing that it is a series of descending and growing patterns. Its defiantly purposeful and complicated."

Angela nodded, "I have been thinking on it too. The first part I got was easy enough to see a pattern in and some co-ordinates but that is the what and where. We need to decipher the why and how of this."

"Well as with any signal from space or ... about space, I figure that is has to be complex by nature," Octan replied. "If it were not, just anybody could decode it. The fact that we can do what we can is impressive, but we literally are mathematically minded. To fully encode it, we need someone that is literally a genius in this stuff."

"It is hard to find someone like that," Angela admitted. "Most people who are publicly able to decode things like this, are very much on the radar and we would have no way of trusting them."

"What if it is someone who would trust us over the alternative?" Octan offered. "Someone who is well versed in the conspiracies and will fear the wrong people knowing as bad as we do?"

"I am not sure I get what you mean," Angela admitted. "Do you have an example?"

"I do in fact," Octan said as he spun his laptop around to show Angela. "This is Dr. Orton Gormanski. He is a master mathematician who worked heavily with NASA in the nineties to invent a new type of propulsion. Per his blog, he got the thing working in simulation, but right before going to practical tests NASA pulled the plug. They not only stopped his research, they sued and discredited him. They claimed that his entire program was fraudulent and got him pretty much railroaded out of the scientific community altogether."

"Normally I would say that was insane ..." Angela answered, remembering holding NASA in such high regard. "But with what I have since seen I am not surprised at all."

"This guy survives now running a blog that tries to expose conspiracies and the like," Octan replied. "Most of what he makes his money at is sensationalism and speculation ... which is why NASA has not yet silenced him. He probably adds more subterfuge to their secrets by the craziness of his theories ... however he is a math genius and literally trained in space technology and messages."

"Are you sure we can trust him?" Angela asked. "We would literally be handing him the keys to everything."

"I am sure we can," Octan replied. "He hates NASA as much as anybody and just to be part of this, I think he'd do just about anything. Besides ... I know the guy ... we go way back."

"He is a friend of yours?" Angela asked. "Like a hacker or professional?"

"Not exactly," Octan replied. "He runs a hobby shop in town in his spare time. I'm a regular."

"So, you want us to go to a comic shop owning blogger who is an ex-NASA theoretical engineer?" Angela asked, summing up the idea which sounded more ridiculous once it was said.

"Pretty much," Octan said with a nod. "Unless you got a better idea."

Angela pondered for a moment, "I actually don't. Let's go see this Dr. Gormanski."

Octan did the work to set up the meeting and Angela took a cab to the location when it was scheduled. The comic shop was called "Prisoners of Gravity" and looked to Angela like every comic shop she had ever seen. It was small and overfilled with books, collectibles, and models, a place that was both alien and strangely comfortable at the same time. As arranged, Angela came at a time the shop was closed and the meeting was to be conducted in private. Though obviously Octan and Gormanski knew each other and Gormanski's name was public that would be all the exchange of names. Angela was introduced as Solitaire and they went right to work once they arrived. Gormanski was younger than Angela had expected, being in his mid-forties and not looking like the old coot she had pictured. He had sandy blonde hair that was swept back with a well-maintained beard that made him look fore like a Starbucks barista than an scientist.

"This better not be a waste of my time," Gormanski said with crossed arms and an obvious air of impatience. "Do you have any idea how often I get fans of the show trying to tell me they have the smoking gun of conspiracies."

"Well all I can ask is for you to take a look," Angela replied, setting up her laptop on a desk nearby that was mostly filled with dungeons and dragons' terrain.

"You know I am very experienced in spotting fakes, photo-shops, and recreations, right?" Gormanski said in his increasingly skeptical tone. "If it weren't for Eugene I would not be making time for this."

Angela shot a look as if saying "Eugene" to Octan before pulling up the recording of the signal for Gormanski. She had prepared but a small part of it for the meeting but enough to show what it was. She stood up and gestured for Gormanski to sit down and take a look at her laptop.

Gormanski sighed, annoyed and sat down but within seconds gasped as he moved closer to hear the tones more accurately.

Octan smiled. "Is it something that ..."

"SHHHHH!" Gormanski said with an urgent finger to his lips. He continued to listen to the recording until the segment ended.

"What do you think?" Angela asked. "Do you believe us now?"

"Never mind that!" Gormanski snapped. "Do you have more?"

***

Gormanski went to work immediately, pouring over the full recording and simply listening to it with no distraction. He wrote nothing down nor did he use any programs to help with his calculations. Angela and Octan waited in the main room, sitting at one of the model tables. Angela tied reading a nearby comic but found herself too distracted to really focus on it.

"He seems to be deep in it," Octan commented with a yawn. "I wonder how long it will take."

"No clue," Angela added. "He is either the genius you suggested or legit crazy. I suppose we will find out soon enough."

Gormanski worked through the night and into the next morning, Angela and Octan napped periodically when they could, but as the sun rose high in the sky, Gormanski stood up suddenly.

"I never had expected to see anything like that!" Gormanski said, surprisingly energetic for a man that just pulled an all-nighter staring at a computer screen. "That is pure brilliance."

"I'm glad you liked it," Angela replied with a tired smile. "Can you tell us what it all means? You didn't write anything down."

"No need, my dear," Gormanski replied with a grin. "For what that is, is something relatively simple."

"Simple?" Octan asked. "How could such a complex series of tones and numbers be something simple?"

Gormanski nodded, waling over to a whiteboard off to the side and wiping magic the gathering tournament brackets off of it. He then proceeded to mark down numbers and letters in no order. "What do you make of this?"

"Letter and numbers," Angela added. "Are they scrambled?"

"Of course they are," Gormanski added. "It may seem like a lot of characters but it is for one thing."

Gormanski rearranged the letters and numbers to spell "1138 Lower Simcoe."

"That's the address of the shop," Octan added.

"This series of numbers is an address?" Angela added. "To what?"

"The earth," Gormanski answered with a grin.

"Why would extra terrestrials be so concerned with the earth's ... address. They seem to already know where it is."

"Knowing where something is does not mean you do not have a purpose for the address," Gormanski explained. "This is not just the basic location of the earth it is a multi-point coordinate that allows for the movement of orbits and an ever-expanding universe. This isn't just an address this is an algorithm to pinpoint exactly where the earth is at any time."

"Why would they need an exact co-ordinate like that?" Angela asked. "What would be so important about it?"

"That I can not be so sure," Gormanski replied. "But it has to do with gravitational shifting and this is probably why they shut me down. If you can figure out the exact place and gravitational calculations of a point in space, then theoretically you could do things to it should you alter that."

"This is a bit too sci-fi for me," Octan added. "Could you explain?"

"This is all the theoretical science you need to understand," Gormanski continued. "But if a space fairing civilization was using something like a gravity drive, they could alter their gravitational forces to move fast or even simultaneously move to a place that has the gravitational position they simulate."

"You mean like they could teleport themselves here or move faster than we could imagine?" Angela speculated.

"In theory, yes," Gormanski replied. "Gravity is one of the most powerful forces in our so-called laws of physics. In theory, they could even use it to create wormholes or literately combine our galaxies into one. There is no way to tell what could be done, but the implications are staggering."

"Do you think NASA is helping them or just trying to copy this technology?" Octan asked. "Either is not something I like the sound of very much."

"That I have no way of knowing," Gormanski added. "We might have looked at all the cards in their hand but only they know the game they are playing."

Angela paused, allowing the ramifications of what she has just heard flow through her head. She had thought it would be something immense but this secret was beyond monumental.

"I have to admit I am surprised on this one," Octan admitted. "I was expecting abductions, resource harvesting, but this? This could mean the end of our entire solar system in an instant."

"Well, we have no way of knowing that is the intention of the aliens," Gormanski added. "To a race that has such profound control over the laws of physics, anything the earth could offer would not seem worth it. They have kept their intentions and very existence a secret so there is no way we can assume they are inherently hostile. For all we know this could just be a study mission."

"We can assume NASA is inherently hostile," Angela replied. "They discredit and even kill to keep their secrets. If the aliens prove harmless, we still must worry about NASA. I saw a woman literally kill herself to protect herself from being seen as a failure."

Octan nodded, "We then have two possibilities ... neither of which I like. First either the aliens are hostile and NASA is working with them to achieve their plan, or that they are not hostile and NASA intends to take advantage of them. Either way the fate of so much rests in the hands of like twelve military guys in a secret room."

"Well, what can we do about it that is the question?" Gormanski asked. "As mentioned we know what they are up to but we don't know what happens next."

"Well we could keep researching," Octan offered. "Go back to the search."

Angela looked out the front window of the shop and watched people walk up and down the street on their way to their daily lives, completely unaware of what was going on around and above them. She knew the truth was no longer out there, they had what was to be discovered and the rest was hidden, only known to a select few. She slowly turned to Octan and Gormanski, "The search is over."

"What do you mean the search is over?" Octan asked in shock. "How can you even expect us to give up knowing what we just learned?"

"I don't expect us to give up," Angela added. "I am just referring to the fact that there is no more searching to do. I have seen the craft. I have seen the cover up. We have the secrets they are hiding and there is nothing more to uncover. Now is the time for action, the time to stare down the dragon in his very den."

"NASA?" Gormanski asked. "You are going to expose them?"

"No," Angela replied with a sigh. "Even if we got CNN to broadcast the signal with the detailed plans of what it was for, it would do very little. As we all know all to well NASA has a very detailed network of lies and distractions and there is no way for people to see through them to the truth of what this is. This is no longer about exposing the secrets. It is about doing what can be done about it and making the sacrifices on what need to be done."

"Well, what do we do then?" Octan asked. "I'm involved in this now and I'm committed for anything."

"As am I," Gormanski added. "You know that I have a score to settle with NASA and I will fight tooth-and-nail if I have to."

Angela smiled, "I could not ask for better friends to face this with.

However, I know what I need to do now and I need to know you two are not involved."

"What do you mean?" Octan asked. "You want us to walk away."

"No," Angela reassured. "I know that would be impossible at this point. I just need to face a lot of the risk alone and I need to know should I come out the other side, that I have people I can trust waiting for me."

"You are going to go alone to NASA, aren't you?" Gormanski asked. "I hope you have a plan."

"You realize, if they see you as a threat you might simply disappear," Octan added.

"I have a plan," Angela reassured. "It is not the best plan, but it is the one I believe has the highest chance of working. I cannot tell it to you as your ignorance of it might be your only protection from the ramifications. I must ask of you to stay silent as long as you can ... keep off the radar for when I need you and be ready to act."

Octan nodded slowly, "I will do it. You can count on me."

"I can't say I like it," Gormanski added. "But I will do the same. I will be ready."

"Good," Angela replied with a smile. "My name is Angela by the way. I just want you to know that I trust you with that and with everything else"

The trio stood for a few moments in silence, letting the ramifications of what was to happen next or could happen eventually sink in. When the group separated, they had no way of knowing of they would ever be gathered again, but could only hope for the best.

***

Angela spent close to a week covering her tracks. She erased everything that might be used to lead to Gormanski or Octan and went over it again and again just to be sure. She wanted to be certain that, should her actions be scrutinized, there would be nothing to indicate she had not acted alone. She flew to Washington and made an appointment with the Director of NASA. She was not surprised to find the meeting was immediately granted, as with many astronauts such a request would likely have to be important. She had never actually met the director, a man simply known as Dr. Enrick, but she knew that if there was a head to this dragon ... he was it.

She entered the NASA headquarters dressed professionally and looking like she was all business. She tried her best to portray an air of confidence as she knew many eyes, both human and digital would be on her the moment she set foot in the building. She was ushered into the meeting room as soon as she arrived and was seated at the end of a long mahogany table. She was alone at one end with a glass of freshly poured water and at the other end was Dr. Enrick and a pair of NASA administrators, both sitting silently to either side.

"So ..." Enrick asked, seemingly not wanting to waste time. "What is the urgent matter you wish to discuss?"

"I'll get right to it," Angela began. "In my many trips to the ISS, I both saw and heard compelling evidence to extra terrestrial activity. I then learned of a cover up and was encouraged not to believe or report what I saw."

Angela reached into her pocket and produced a thumb drive with the recording on it. She slid it down the table to Enrick who picked it up and slid it into a tiny laptop. He kept an eye on Angela, offering no reaction or emotional response to what she was saying. He looked over the file as it displayed then looked back up to Angela.

"This is a recording of the alien signal being broadcast from orbit," Angela added. "It is the only copy and I retrieved it at great lengths and danger in South America. I deciphered it and know that it is an algorithm that exactly dictates the gravitational location of the earth in the cosmos. I know that you already have this signal and know about the alien presence."

"I see," Enrick replied in a neutral tone. "What is it that you are hoping to accomplish? Do you presume to expose us?"

"Not at all," Angela replied. "Had I wanted to expose this cover up I would have done so already. There is no smoking gun, no broadcasting of this, the secret still stands undiscovered by the mainstream populace."

Enrick leaned forward on his elbows, linking his fingers through each other, "Then what is it that you want?"

"Simple," Angela replied with a smile. "I want in."

CHAPTER THREE
From the Inside

Angela had no way of knowing if her risky gambit would work. The idea that Enrick would trust her was a long shot and she knew it. However, the benefit of someone like her on their side seemed to far outweigh the risk involved. With the power that NASA wielded, it was no trouble to silence her after the fact should she prove unworthy. She was allowed into an area in the NASA headquarters she never knew existed. In her long years with NASA she had never even heard such a facility and was surprised to find it so involved. It was known simply as the backlog; named simply so if it showed up on documents, it would seem like a small archive and not worthy of a second glance. However, it was a fortified facility where NASA could do clandestine experiments and hold their secrets in safety. As Angela was given level one clearance all she could really do was get into the barracks, cafeteria, and meeting rooms. She was warned what would happen should she try and go anywhere beyond her clearance.

For the first week or so it was just meetings and waiting. No one seemed to know what to do with Angela and did not want to trust her with much. They kept dropping off things for her to review, but most were paper transcripts of long conversations from oversight communities ... nothing secretive or even consequential. Angela was starting to think she had made a big mistake when someone new came to see her. He was a tall man of Indian decent with slick black hair and a rugged demeanour. He was well dressed and had an air of confidence about him.

"You are Angela, right?" the man asked her. "You want to get some real work done?"

"Absolutely!" Angela said, looking up from her most recent notes about a budget meeting for a project that was cancelled right after. "What do you need?"

"Good, good," the man replied. "You may call me Mr. Stone. I will be your ... handler of sorts when we need things of you."

"Sounds good Mr. Stone," Angela said with a nod.

"Now keep in mind I expect great things and even greater obedience," Mr. Stone explained. "You bring me results and you will be rewarded. You cross me or fail, you will find worse things then remedial reviewing of outdated documents."

"Understood," Angela said with a nod. "I will endeavour to exceed your expectations."

"That is what I want to hear," Stone replied. "Follow me."

Angela got up and followed Stone to one of the empty meeting rooms. He gestured for her to sit and plugged a personal device into the view screen and brought up some information. On the screen were pictures of some manner of business.

"This is BriarTech," Stone began. "A multi faceted technology business that works in both hardware and software."

"I have heard of them," Angela replied. "They do a lot of different things. I think I had one of their tablets once."

"Indeed," Stone replied. "They have had a lot of success but are venturing into our neighborhood and it is causing us concern."

"Practically or in theory?" Angela asked. "Like, are they rivalling some of our technology or trying to find out something we know?"

"A little of both I'm afraid," Stone replied. "Their new devices that are coming onto the market can catalogue information on a rather hard to control scale. In theory, they could use this technology to control the existing satellite system to compartmentalize information that we do not want known."

Angela thought back to her research on the deep web and conspiracy theories and remembered one about using such a network as a kind of compiled antenna to get information from space.

"You think they can use this to monitor space without us being able to regulate it?" Angela asked. "A kind of guerrilla space radio receiver."

"Very good," Stone said with a perked eyebrow. "You are quite good at seeing the patterns. We are in fact certain that they are going to use this network to monitor space freely and we can't have them do that."

Angela nodded, "We can't allow such free and unfettered access to space to fall into civilian hands."

"Exactly," Stone nodded. "We need to shut them down ... not just now, but cripple their ability to even attempt anything like this from happening again."

"How exactly do we do that?" Angela asked.

"That is where you come in," Stone replied as he slid a thumb drive onto the desk in front of Angela. "This needs to be uploaded into the private server in their headquarters in San Francisco."

"What is this, like a super-virus?" Angela asked as she picked up the thumb drive.

"Nothing so pedantic," Stone replied. "Viruses are child's play and companies that get hit by them bounce back fast and illicit public sympathy. No one likes to get hit by a virus and will forgive a business just as they would forgive a friend for getting hit."

"Then what is it?" Angela asked.

"It is a doctored directory of personal correspondence within the company," Stone replied. "Fake emails and messages from top ranking employees to each other. They are a mix of racist comments, offensive tirades and other socially problematic discussions."

"It will just put them on the server?" Angela asked.

"This is a simple program that will insert these files into the server so they cannot be distinguished from real messages," Stone explained. "Once in, we will have one of our hackers break into the system copy a large chunk of their messages ... this included and 'leak' them to the press."

"The public outcry against them will be instantaneous," Angela replied, finding herself quite frightened by the creativity NASA had at it's disposal. "It will immediately ruin their reputation."

Stone smiled, "With no way to prove they aren't legitimate and with so much evidence they were on their server, they will have no defence. Even trying to deny it will make them look worse. The only recourse will be to fire everyone who supposedly sent the messages."

"I presume they are all the people on the space network project,"

Angela guessed.

"Exactly," Stone replied. "It will cripple the project and put the entire company back ten years. If they ever even THINK about doing anything like it again, we will remind the public about this ... embarrassing incident."

"It's a fantastic plan," Angela replied. Even though she was terrified by it, she admitted it was fascinating in its scope. "How should I get it on their server?"

"That is up to you," Stone replied. "We will arrange your flight to San Francisco ... how you get it there ... is all on you. Your resourcefulness and skill is what we are gauging this on. Consider this as your chance to prove not only your trustworthiness, but your worth."

"I won't let you down," Angela said with a nod, her mind already scrambling for plans on how she would get the mission done.

Twenty-four hours later, Angela was in San Francisco and ready to set her plan in motion. She had wracked her brain on the flight over and something she had read about cyber crime occurred to her. She knew that even the most infallible computer systems had one major flaw ... the user. She recalled that once there was a virus called "Stuxnet" that found its way into an Iranian uranium enrichment center and it caused the automated centrifuges to spin out of control and nearly caused a disaster. The thing of it was that the site was completely off the communications grid ... the virus being accidentally brought in by a discarded thumb drive that was planted as a trap. This was Angela's best idea to get the information into the place. However, she knew that most of the people working there would be careful so she needed to prepare some things and pick her target just right. She used cash to hire a local photographer and got some nice clothes and a wig from a shop. She had the photographer take a series of sexy photos of her at various landmarks. Angela admitted to herself that she did not usually do things like this, but it was kinda fun to try it. Once she received the photos she added them to the hard drive along with the pictures. She was careful not to damage the data, having brief instructions to how the thumb drive was set up.

With the pictures done she went to a coffee shop across the street from the BriarTech corporate headquarters. She sat down with a laptop with a close lookout for just the right target. Soon enough a lonely looking manager with a BriarTech name badge came down to get coffee. Angela caught him looking at her and knew she had his attention. She was dressed in a tight red dress with black high heels and she was hoping for just this kind of attention. She acted quickly and got to work on her planned performance.

"Damned computer!" Angela said as she smacked the laptop she brought. "Why won't this thing ever work?"

"Perhaps I could be of some assistance?" the BriarTech businessman said as he walked over, nervously holding his coffee in both hands. "I work for a computer company."

"Oh, that would be great," Angela replied in her best damsel in distress voice. "Are you like one of those Bill Jobs type geniuses?"

"Well no, not really," the man replied before pausing. "Well ... actually, yes I am. What seems to be the problem?"

"Oh, just my vacation photo-shoot pictures," Angela replied. "Paid the photographer and we shot, but all he gave me was this blasted thumb drive. The pictures are on there but I have no idea how to get them out. I'd go to like a tech but they are ... a little bit saucy."

"Well, let me give it a shot," the man replied as he gestured for her to move over and let him try the laptop. Angela stepped aside and let him go to work. She had set the laptop to not immediately recognize USB device and hoped this would lead the man to believe that she was in fact just too dumb to do it manually. Within seconds he had it open and pictures were going up on the screen, as planned sexy pictures that would stick in his mind.

"Oh, you did it!" Angela said with a smile. "You really are a genius!"

"Well, I do OK," the man replied, transfixed by the pictures. "You look like you ... had fun."

Angela repressed her urge to cringe as she looked at her phone, "Oh no! I'm late for my tour group. Gotta go!"

She quickly packed up her laptop and made a big fuss as she stuffed it in her bag, "Thanks for everything!"

"My ... pleasure," the man replied as Angela rushed out of the coffee shop. She made one look back at the thumb drive she intentionally left on the table and watched as the lonely man picked it up and put it in his pocket. As Angela got out of sight she sighed a sigh of relief. There was no way that guy would wait till he got home to look at more photos on that thumb drive.

Angela went back to her hotel and she no way to know if her cunning plan would work. She decided to wait a couple of days to see if her ruse was successful, lest she need to try it again. Sure enough, two days later in the morning when she turned on the television in her room the headline was about BriarTech. She turned up the volume in time to hear a newscaster explain the story.

"We come back to our developing story out of BriarTech. The tech giant was rocked today when a whistle-blower close to the company released hundreds of emails and interoffice memos showing overt racism, preferential treatment, and sexual extortion. Stock for the company has dipped drastically and the CEO of BriarTech has promised immediate dismissals for all employees involved. This is expected to delay or derail their launch of ..."

Angela was interrupted as her phone went off, she quickly picked it up and put it to her ear, "Hello?"

"Excellent work," Stone said in a happy tone. "You have done well ... come back as soon as you can ... we have much to discuss."

Angela ended the call and smiled. She felt bad for what she had done but knew that it was part of her plan. If she was going to stop NASA, she had to act like them ... she had to get her hands dirty.

***

By the time Angela got back to the backlog, the BriarTech situation devolved from PR scandal to full blown corporate catastrophe. There were talks of stock plunges and even talk of a rival company, Ulta-con, buying the fledgling tech giant and re-branding it. Angela knew her subterfuge was only the tip of the iceberg and knew that NASA had sunk its teeth deeply into the neck of the company. She had once thought the agency to be focused on exploration and discovery and wanted so desperately to know what happened to it ... how had it become this secret consortium of lies and deception.

Stone was waiting for her as she arrived and presented her with her level two clearance. This would get her past the rather rudimentary area of level one and into the next area ... the analysts. Angela was presented with a cubicle in a massive computer room filled with people working silently on their machines.

"I must say you really impressed us," Stone replied with a grin. "The stranded model routine ... pure genius."

"I am not surprised you were watching me," Angela replied. "I presumed as much actually."

"Such is the nature of our operation," Stone replied. "Assume everything will go sideways on you all the time and be pleasantly surprised when something does not."

"So, what do I do now?" Angela asked. "I presume I will actually be doing real operations now."

"You're on the next rung of the ladder, my dear," Stone replied. "Here we are going to need to see if you can find meaning in the chaos."

"I am not entirely sure what that is?" Angela asked in a curious tone.

"This is the crucible," Stone replied. "Here we use machines nearly untraceable in the outside world and we watch and we listen."

"Like the NSA?" Angela asked. "Looking for potential threats?"

Stone laughed, "The NSA peeks in at teenagers' Facebooks and logs gigaquads of information. They have no clue on how to even sort it. Here, we are hunters. Elite searchers for those real threats and problems before they come around to bite us."

"You want me to find out people who have ... information they should not have?" Angela asked.

"Precisely," Stone replied. "If it is something simple like a kid with a website with something he shouldn't ... get one of the administrators to get him banned from his server. If it is something serious however ... like the BriarTech situation ... you bring it to me."

"This is what you want me doing?" Angela asked in a skeptical tone. "You saw me in the field ... I can do so much more."

"Oh, we know," Stone admitted. "Though you must admit that your skill set and loyalty seems too good to be true. We need to try you on different levels to make sure you are the ... real deal. Get us a smoking gun ... something juicy and we will see about what else we can have you do."

"I will not let you down," Angela said with an encouraging nod. "I will land the big fish."

"That is what I want to hear," Stone said before dismissing himself and heading off.

For the next few days Angela poked around with the computers and found them to be technological marvels. She would follow a Facebook link and the computer would log her in as some sort of super-admin. She found that she could delete, alter, or add anything she wanted to several prominent sites. She thought back to Octan and wondered how much fun he would have on such a network. She admitted she missed her partner in crime but was glad to keep him safely out of NASA's clutches. Angela found it weird to be on the other side. At the beginning of everything, she was desperately searching for alien information that was being hidden from the public. However, now she was searching some the same information but to take it from the public and silence it. However, the old problem persisted, she was lost in a sea of crackpots and click-bait artists and it was difficult to find any truth. As day after day went by she began to feel more and more frustrated, her clandestine mission had halted and she did not want to be stuck in the analyst pit forever.

"How do I even know what they are not even supposed to know," Angela said out loud. "It's like trying to guard a net and you don't know where the players are."

"Why don't you consult the blacklist?" a female voice asked from the cubicle next to her.

Angela moved to see an Asian girl sitting in the next stall. She was dressed in a white blouse, black skirt but with her shoes off and put up on the desk. Her workstation was cluttered with Star Wars collectibles and did not seem to be a pace where any serious work got done.

"Uh, hi," Angela said in an awkward tone. "I'm Angela ... I just got here a few days back."

"I'm Hina," the girl replied. "I've been here for ... like forever. I heard you are the one who put the email on the hard drive of BriarTech. I was the one who wrote the algorithm to buy it in their systems!"

"Pleased to meet you Hina," Angela said with a smile. "What did you mean by blacklist?"

"Oh, it is a document listing current secrets and terms we are not supposed to let people talk about," Hina explained. "You should be able to get to it on drive J on your computer. You cannot copy or move anything from it and, any time you open it or read it, they log it."

"Can you show me?" Angela asked, shocked that NASA had such a document. "They keep all the secrets in there?"

"Not all," Hina replied as she brought up the drive and it started displaying files on the screen. "Mostly just the government level stuff ... they have stuff beyond us, but that is in a higher clearance grade. Take this for example. They have an animal disease control centre on Plum Island in New York State. It is actually a chemical weapon testing plant and like every couple of weeks, we got to cover up some kind of local mishap."

"Mishap?" Angela asked in shock, not realizing how Hina could be so caviller about such a thing.

"Well, I can't say why or how, but it seems that the aging facility has been unable to contain the stuff they do there," Hina said. "Though they also might be testing things."

"Are you OK with things like that?" Angela asked. "Testing viruses on people and such?"

"Well it's not so black and white, right?" Hina commented. "Like, if they are doing stuff like that there must be a good reason, right?"

"They ever told you what that reason was?" Angela asked.

"No," Hina admitted. "That is a level five kinda thing."

"What else is in there?" Angela asked. "Are we like allowed to talk about this blacklist?"

"Oh totally," Hina admitted. "They don't let people into level two if they don't trust them with what is in the blacklist. The stuff in it is mostly conspiracies that are out there and we need to keep in mind if anyone gains any real notice or has any evidence. What they really want is people who have something new and exciting. That is really hard to find."

"Tell me about it," Angela said. "All I can find is people who think they saw a Chacarera."

"Chacareras are totally real," Hina replied. "There's a farm of them in South America."

"You are joking, right?" Angela asked with a perked eyebrow.

Hina opened another file in the blacklist that showed information about an instillation in South America that in fact bred chacareras.

"I'll be damned," Angela said with a nod.

"But you are right," Hina replied. "There is a lot of chafe out there. We should know ... this department is responsible for skewing the search engines. However, we are also supposed to be finding threats and we are literally making our own job harder for ourselves. If you get a lead and you need help, you let me know."

Angela nodded. She needed an ally in NASA and the girl seemed to be blissfully unaware of the dangers she was helping hide ... however, this also meant that she was not just blindly devoted to NASA either. Perhaps if she helped her, she could gain her trust for things to come ... even if they are anti-NASA. The real trouble moving forward was that Angela was not close to any real kind of breakthrough. She wished she had Octan's help and that got her thinking. He had been successful on the deep web and perhaps they could be again. It was quite a curious thing and she wanted to discover was how much of a presence the network had there.

"Hina," Angela asked. "Do you ever search the deep web?"

"Not really," Hina admitted. "It is just too chaotic and hard to moderate. NASA tried to shut it down once and found it pointless. The amount of people who actually go on there is relatively small so they just kinda ignore it."

"Well I found evidence there and it's what got me in the door here,"

Angela replied. "Perhaps you can help me search."

Hina shrugged, "I can get the network to connect to it fine, but I can't guarantee anyone will really care what we find there."

"We won't know until we look," Angela said with a nod.

Over the next two days Hina and Angela worked together to find some semblance of worthy information in the deep web. As with before, it was a disorganized place but it seemed like they might be getting somewhere. Angela was staying late, her eyes glazing over from staring at a screen all day. She got to a strange list of things listed by an anonymous poster.

"Hey Hina?" Angela asked out load. "Can I run some tags past you to see if anything is real?"

"Go for it," Hina replied in a bored tone.

"OK let's see," Angela began. "Space weapon tests, abduction from eastern Europe, a second sun, something about a space amoeba."

"Did you say second sun?" Hina said, swivelling over and considering Angela's cubicle. "That is of interest?"

"That the earth has a second sun?" Angela scoffed. "That is probably the weirdest conspiracy theory I have ever heard of."

"Even so, it is a code-word I heard Stone saying once," Hina replied. "This is potentially big."

"Do we have any way of knowing who posted this?" Angela asked. "This site logs no personal information beyond a handle."

"This is kinda a specialty of mine," Hina said as she took over Angela's workstation. "I wrote an algorithm to look over all posts by a specific anonymous user even if it is with a handle. He may give no information, but all his posts are linked together as his own. The program looks for key information with his grammar, common used words and anything that only certain people would know. For example, it is already showing me multiple grammatical mistakes of someone with an eastern European accent where English is not their native tongue. I would imagine Austrian or Russian. Also, his typos are consistent with an intellectual ... someone typing slower than their brain can keep up with. I'd imagine a doctor or scientist."

"You can get all this from message board posts?" Angela asked in shock.

"Totally," Hina replied. "And there is more. He refers to things from the book series 'Dune' three times. In fact, his handle is from the same series. I am cross referencing forums for 'Dune' and his handle."

"How close do you think we can get with this?" Angela asked, still slightly skeptical she would get any real information.

"His name is Vlad Pitrosen and he is from Crimea," Hina said proudly. "Ex-Russian cosmonaut and current radar technician for a private astronomy firm in Moscow. I have cross referenced accounts on fourteen different services and made up a pattern to link them all the way back to the deep web."

"That is amazing!" Angela replied, glad that this woman had not stumbled across Octan and Angela when they were searching or they would have been caught for sure. "Should I send this to Stone?"

"Please do," Hina replied. "Make sure though that my name is on it as well."

Angela nodded and sent the information to Stone in an email. Within moments the back door opened up and Stone walked into the room. He stopped between Hina and Angela's desk.

"Good work my friends," Stone said politely. "Welcome to level three ... Also, how would you both like to visit Moscow? I heard it is quite nice this time of year ..."

***

It, in fact, was not nice in Moscow that time of year. It was cold and already snowing by the time Hina and Angela got to their hotel. Their cover was that they were university bloggers and NASA had provided them with frighteningly accurate credentials. The school that they were even supposed to represent had called ahead ... on NASA's orders, to set up the meeting to add an extra level of authenticity. The pair dressed as students ... under many levels of cold weather gear and headed to the radar array that Vlad worked at. After spending so much time in NASA and its cutting-edge facilities, it was a stark contrast to see the only building and outdated technology. Angela could not help but be reminded of the archaic Frankenstein technology of the radar array in South America when she looked around. It was impressive by the fact that they could seemingly get results with what they had to work with.

Soon enough Angela and Hina were in a small office, waiting for the interview and getting ready.

"This is so exciting!" Hina said in a jovial tone. "I can't believe we are here."

"That's great," Angela replied with a noticeably more cautious tone. "Remember our cover though. We have to find out what this guy knows without letting him know who we are."

"Right!" Hina said with a nod. "How do I do that?"

Angela sighed, starting to doubt how useful Hina would be under this situation. "I think you better let me do the talking."

Vlad came in and introduced himself. He was a middle-aged man with grey hair and an expanding mid-section. He looked tired and overworked and altogether disinterested in the prospects of an article.

"So, you ... are both interested in radar engineering?" Vlad asked with a perked eyebrow.

Hina went to talk but Angela silenced her with a sideways look. Instead Hina took out her phone and started looking at it.

Angela smiled to the man. "Oh yes. Though it is a technology that many think is outdated we know that there are countless applications in the private sector of ..."

"You work for NASA then?" Vlad asked suddenly. "You want to know what I know."

"No!" Angela lied. "We are just here to do an article."

"There are literally a thousand better places to go that are not so cold," Vlad commented. "I have nothing to tell you."

"Actually, you do," Hina replied. "I just cloned your phone and see that you have been talking about some rather interesting stuff."

"You what?" Vlad asked. "My phone? But it's in Russian."

"Oh, you think that since I'm Japanese, that I can't speak Russian?" Hina scoffed. "I learn languages for fun. I mastered Latin in a weekend. You think I can't read Russian? So, who is she anyway?"

"That is none of your business!" Vlad started, but stopped. "What is it you want?"

"Information," Angela responded, following Hina's lead. "You seem to already know what we are looking for. Tell us about the second sun."

Vlad sighed, "All right. A few years ago, a radio telescope was doing a live broadcast of a planet's silhouette crossing the sun. There was a reflection from the lens and someone on the live chat link asked about it. The host remarked that it was the secret second sun of the solar system and then moved on. It was meant as a wry remark but happened to touch on a NASA conspiracy. There is an orbital ... anomaly that might call for another planet or star that might be on a very far elliptical orbit through our solar system. It might not come through our orbits for thousands of years at a time. This is something NASA does not want becoming public knowledge for some reason and they shut it all down."

"Interesting," Angela commented. "But that is what happened before. Tell us what you know now that makes you so important."

"Why do you even need to know anyway?" Vlad asked. "Don't people like me who know too much just ... disappear."

"Not necessarily," Angela replied. "You are being quite co-operative and people who cooperate are not usually needing to be ... censored. Or are you deciding to become difficult?"

Vlad took a deep breath, "I will tell you everything. Have you ever heard of the Bilderberg group?"

"Enlighten me," Angela asked, not having any idea what he was talking about.

"They are a group of powerful bankers, industrialists, politicians, and even world leaders," Vlad began. "They started meeting years ago to discuss political trends and secret back door treaties. However, as years went by and the success of the meetings grew, their purview intensified. They began to play with things on a grand scale and this is part of who ultimately pulls the strings in the secret world. Who do you think funds your precious NASA?"

"We know this," Angela said, trying to sound aloof and keep him intimidated. "Where is the part that would interest us?"

"I am getting to it," Vlad assured. "Ever since NASA shut down the people involved with the second sun speculation, many people have gotten together to secretly deliver information NASA desperately wants hidden. They appropriately named themselves ... the Second Sun."

"This group has been a thorn in our side," Angela replied, pretending she knew more about them then she did.

"I can imagine so," Vlad confirmed. "I am only a casual member, but I see members suddenly disappear. I feared too deep an involvement. However, since you are here, I suppose that I was right to be afraid."

"You are getting off topic," Angela warned.

"You are right," Vlad replied. "The information that I had the ... misfortune of seeing, is that the Second Sun confirmed that the location of the next meeting of the Bilderberg group has changed and as has the date that meeting will take place."

"And when would that be?" Angela asked in a coy tone, pretending she was skeptical as to if he had the right information."

"A month from now on the fourth," Vlad replied. "In NASA headquarters in Washington. Something called the ... backlog."

"What is it you know about this meeting?" Angela asked. "Remember, now is not the time to get vague."

"I know that this is an urgent meeting and not one of their usual ones," Vlad replied. "It looks as though something is happening and it's spooked them. There was speculation as to what, but the only clue we have is NASA doubling down on censoring anything mentioning the Second Sun. Some mentions about something called Project Nemesis."

"What do you know about Project Nemesis?" Angela asked ... pretending she had even heard of it.

"No clue," Vlad replied. "That I promise you. We have been trying to find out what it is but that one is a tough nut to crack."

"I believe you," Angela replied with a smile. She realized the man was terrified and growing more and more on edge. She didn't really care how much he knew, but figured this was enough to prove her worth to NASA. She began to think of no evasive ways she could pitch to Stone to silence the man. He seemed a nice enough person and really did not want to ruin his life unless she absolutely had to.

"What happens now?" Vlad asked nervously.

"Well, you co-operated," Angela said, standing up and gesturing Hina to follow her. "That will go a long way."

"But we know everything," Hina added. "So, you better start pretending you know nothing."

"Of course," Vlad said, allowing both women to pass him and leave the room.

In the adjoining hallway, Angela and Hina started putting on their coats to prepare for the weather beyond.

"That was amazing," Angela commented to Hina. "How did you clone his phone? What was he hiding?"

"I didn't," Hina replied with a grin. "Cloning a phone is really difficult to do so easily and it would take me hours to decipher anything good from it. I just played the laws of averages. He's a middle-aged guy with no wedding ring. Everyone has something messed up on their phone and figured he might be as well."

"You were bluffing?" Angela said in an impressed tone. "Very nice."

"This is my first try at field work," Hina replied proudly. "I must say I like it and …"

Hina was interrupted by a gunshot going off in the room they just left. Hina crumpled to the ground instinctively while Angel cautiously moved to check what had happened.

"Dear God," Angela muttered as she saw a grizzly scene before her.

"What is it?" Hina asked, looking up from where she was crouched.

"It's Vlad," Angela replied, trying to reconcile a horrific sight for the second time. "He shot himself."

Angela and Hina fled the scene. NASA seemed to have a cleanup crew waiting and standing by. Hina seemed to be in a state of shock and Angela took her back to the hotel to calm her down.

"I ... I killed him," Hina said in a shocked tone. "I didn't mean to."

"You didn't kill him," Angela said as she slid down to sit with Hina. "He had secrets and wanted to die to keep them secret. They would have come out eventually anyway and he made a choice."

"Is this what you were talking about?" Hina asked. "The people that we didn't know are getting hurt."

"Kinda, yeah," Angela replied.

"I hate it," Hina replied. "I hate it now that I have seen in in person."

"Kind of makes it hard to ignore," Angela replied. "Believe me I have seen my share."

"I don't know if I can go back," Hina replied.

"You can," Angela said, crouching down and leaning close. "There is a greater good involved and on this you can trust me. You might not see it now, but if you come back, keep working with me ... I promise to show it to you."

"You promise?" Hina said, looking up with desperate eyes.

"I promise," Angela assured. "Trust me and everything will eventually be all right."

***

NASA had proven quite skilled at covering up what had happened. The suicide did not show up on the news and instead Vlad was listed as "retired." Angela did not like that this was the second person in so many weeks that had killed themselves over the protection of secrets. She admitted that she had a greater understanding of this now. Remembering Octan and realizing that some secrets were worthy of protecting. As Hina and Angela got back to the backlog, they were treated like returning salesmen that landed a big sale. The information from Vlad had been legitimate and links on his devices lead to tracking down a lot of the Second Sun's secret network. Angela and Hina were given level four clearance and now had their own offices side by side. Angela was surprised to find that now her computer had access to a treasure trove of secrets. She could not even begin to go through it all. All manner of proof and information on cover-ups and conspiracies were at her fingertips. However as tempting as any of this information was, it was not what she wanted. The signal in space and things related to it were noticeably absent. It had to be behind closed doors with only the top brass knowing of it all. Any of the smaller things might raise problems but not one of them were worth exposing herself as a double agent.

The main thing, the big fish was the Bilderberg meeting. Angela knew this had something to do with the signal from space and she had to find out what went on there. Given her clearance she was able to confirm that the meeting was happening. It was listed on the date and part of her job, and the others were to suppress any information of the people coming. There was a partial list of attendees available and it was literally a laundry list of some of the most powerful people in the world. Angela had to find a way to either attend the meeting or hear it. She decided that she needed Hina's help if she was going to accomplish it.

Angela went to Hina's new office and found her on her computer going through the now declassified files, "Mind if I bother you Hina?"

"Oh, of course," Hina said, welcoming her into the room. "You can come sit with me and go over some files."

"Um. OK," Angela said, pulling up a chair and sitting down.

Once seated, Hina reached out and touched her phone, "There ... I think we should be good now."

"Good now?" Angela asked. "I don't understand."

"I discovered this morning that this room is audio monitored," Hina said. "I figured I needed a way to make it so I could talk freely, so I made a database of my random noises and sounds and made a program that would intercept the outgoing audio and replace it with those sounds. It also sorts them into random orders so it is near impossible to tell they aren't live."

"That's amazing," Angela replied. "You did this just today?"

"It wasn't that hard," Hina replied. "But after all that ... stuff in Russia, I figured I might need the ability to talk in private."

"Good, because I need your help as I might need to circumvent some level five stuff."

"The Bilderberg meeting!" Hina replied. "You want to see it, don't you?"

Angela paused. She knew she was hoping Hina was coming to her side after the Moscow incident, but part of her was concerned it might be a trap. However, she knew that if she were to get any information on the meeting she would need Hina. She was at the point of her investigation where she needed to take a risk in order to get a reward. "Can you get me into it?"

"Not you specifically," Hina replied. "But I can get us a live feed."

"OK!" Angela said with an encouraged nod. "How do we do that?"

"Well, some of the security measures are known at this level," Hina admitted. "The guests are all supposed to disable their phones even before they get here ... however, I know for a fact that there is at least one attendee of the meeting that won't have theirs off."

"Who?" Angela asked, liking the plan forming before her.

"Mr. Stone," Hina replied. "He has this compulsion with his phone and I know he never turns it off for any reason."

"Wouldn't his phone be like super-secure?" Angela asked, but Hina just looked up at with a look of surprise as if she could not believe that Angela would think she could not crack it. Angela shrugged. "You're right ... how do we do it."

"Well, this place does have WiFi and he definitely uses it a lot," Hina replied. "Even people like him who are concerned with security will use WiFi when available. There actually are several in here and he is connected to a private one."

"Can we get on that one?" Angela asked. "Without being monitored?"

"That is the challenge," Hina replied. "I can make any number of devices break into that network. However, the second they do, an alarm will go off. However, if you can get close enough to Mr. Stone's phone I can register his information. Basically, I can build a way to make his phone connect to not just the private WiFi, but the regular one as well. From there I can turn on the microphone to his phone and broadcast it to us."

"You can remotely make someone phone record audio?" Angela asked in shock.

"We're NASA," Hina replied as she pressed several buttons on her keyboard. "I just used your phones camera to take a picture of your pocket."

"That is amazing," Angela commented. "Let's get to work."

It took a couple of days for Hina to get everything working and for them to secretly test it. Everything seemed to work perfectly but the next step was to be the most challenging. Angela needed to talk to Mr. Stone and keep his focus for the sixty seconds it would take for her phone to interact with his. She caught up with him in the hallway.

"Mr. Stone do you have a minute?" Angela said as she walked up, knowing her phone would start trying to connect when she became within five feet of Stone.

"I am a little busy now I am afraid," Stone replied. "I don't have much more than a minute at all today."

"I will be quick," Angela said. "I wonder who I would talk to about going into the field on something."

"You have a lead?" Stone asked with a perked eyebrow.

"It may be nothing," Angela admitted. "It might be a wild goose chase but I think it is worth a try."

"Well, I suppose you might want to wait until you are sure," Stone said reaching his hand into his pocket. Angela had to act fast as it would show an icon that his phone was being connected to if he was looking at it as her phone worked. "I think it might be someone who calculated the trajectory of the supposed second sun."

Stone paused, stopping going from his phone, "That is important. Tell you what ... wait until things die down, after the VIPs leave and you can take Hina and any other resources you need."

"That would be great," Angela admitted. "Thank you so much."

"You are doing good work for us and we are very impressed," Stone admitted. "We might even need you to go up again. We need some eyes in space coming up."

"You will have them," Angela smiled, realizing she had not recently thought about her main dream, it becoming lost in the chaos. Angela realized it had been long enough and the connection was done. "Don't let me keep you from your business ... I can only imagine what you have to do."

"You have no idea," Stone said with a smile before excusing himself and heading off.

On the day of the meeting Hina and Angel waited in Hina's office. They had made a lot of preparations and were waiting for the meeting to begin.

"OK I have the audio jamming in place and both of our laptops are configured to be on the network simulating work we are doing. If anyone checks up on us we seemed very busy. However, it also will broadcast the meeting live for us."

"Perfect," Angela commented. "I can't even imagine what they are going to say in there."

The link was made and audio began. The first hour or so were formalities and talks of matters unrelated to NASA or anything Angela was interested in ... however, things changed as Enrick arrived and began to speak.

"I am sorry to cut the usual maters short," Enrick began. "But there is a certain matter that requires our immediate attention."

Angela and Hina could hear the room grow quiet, everyone seeming very eager to hear what Enrick had to say.

"As you know there are developments in Project Nemesis," Enrick began. "We have been in contact with ... our benefactors for some time and the next phase of the turntable is coming to fruition. The technology being shared with humanity is close to being practical and things will get very ... exciting very soon. Nemesis is coming and soon the need for secrecy will be over. However, until that time we need to step up our game. If the public got wind of what we are doing now, it could seriously jeopardize our plans."

"What do you propose?" an unfamiliar voice asked. "You will have any help from me that you need."

"That is very fortunate," Enrick added. "I will take you up on that. I was hoping that you and Mr. Ryan would join us in the inner archive."

"We would be honored," the unfamiliar voice replied. "I presume I speak for you as well."

"Of course," the supposed Mr. Ryan added. "I am honoured to be chosen."

"Excellent," Enrick replied. "We will go down in the morning. It is an honor to be chosen and you both have earned it."

"Have we had any developments on the so called Second Sun group?" another voice spoke up. "I fear they might not be the crackpots we thought they were."

"We have had some recent luck in weeding some of them out," Enrick replied. "We wiped out a secret cell of them in Russia. Now that BriarTech has been silenced and the array in South America is being dismantled they have no way to truly monitor us now. Anything further will be them playing with information and secrets that will soon be too late to be used to stop what we are planning."

"This has been in the works for far too long," another voice interjected. "There is so much at stake."

"It will be worth it, I assure you," Enrick replied. "Our benefactors want so very much from us and soon we will all get exactly as we want ... and what we deserve."

After this the business went back to political and business dealings and soon the group was dismissed. Hina terminated the signal now that it was no longer needed.

"I did not understand half of that," Hina admitted. "What do we do now?"

"I'm not entirely sure," Angela admitted. "Though I really think we need to find out how to get into this ... archive. Whatever they are going to do to those two ... volunteers ... can't be good. It might be the answer to all of this."

"OK," Hina nodded. "I will do what I can before tomorrow morning to get you in there."

"I believe in you," Angela nodded in encouragement, though deep down all she could feel was apprehension and fear for the ramifications of what she had heard."

***

Angela got up and early in the backlog and readied herself as she thought of what was likely to occur. She had taken an increasing amount of risks but today was going to be a big one. She was in a den of vipers and about to do something that might expose her completely. As nervousness and dread formed within her chest, Angela fought it back. This was precisely why she was here, exactly why she left her friends and stopped fighting from the shadows. There were answers in this archive room in level five and she wanted nothing more then to get them. She had no way of knowing how she was even going to accomplish her task. She had learned that Hina had an uncanny way of surmounting challenges. She decided that if they managed to get in and out of this mysterious room that she would let her into all their plans on the outside. Angela could not allow herself too much thought about things beyond her current mission ... she needed to keep the idea of what there was to lose to the back of her head lest it cloud her judgment.

Angela found distraction about thinking about the wonderful plan that Hina had come up with as she came to her office. The normally jovial woman stood there with a worried look on her face. She quickly set the jamming program.

"Were you not able to do it?" Angela asked, admitting part of her would be relieved if that was so. "Can we not go in?"

"We can do it," Hina replied. "But it is a pretty rough plan and a stupid risk."

"Let's hear it then," Angela said with a nod. "Stupid risks seem to be my foray as of late."

"Well, you ever see a bad movie where someone crawls through a vent to get through a building?" Hina asked.

"There is no way there are people sized vents in this building?" Angela asked skeptically.

"We're underground so there so very much are," Hina replied. "The real thing is that in reality no one is really fit enough to crawl through vents like that. The upper body strength alone ..."

"I can do it," Angela replied. "That will be no problem."

"Yeah you do work out ... like a lot," Hina agreed.

"Aren't there like security measures and such?" Angela added. "There aren't lasers are there?"

"Lasers?" Hina asked. "Why would there be lasers?"

"I don't know," Angela replied. "Like to keep people out."

"Lasers don't work that way," Hina replied. "Though there is a complex system of alarms and sound censors."

"How are we getting around those?" Angela asked. "I presume you have a plan for that."

"Yeah but it's a tight one," Hina nodded. "I hacked into a work order this morning and changed a breaker that will be pulled. It will look like a clerical error, but it will mean that the alarms in the vents will be off. I also added two other places that will get pulled so it won't be so obvious what we we're after if they do suspect sabotage. However, there is a very real chance that the system will recognize that something is off that shouldn't be and set off an alarm. If that happens the facility will go into lock-down. If you are still in the vent when that happens you will be stuck ... which is monumentally bad. If you are still on your way back here, you will be stranded ... which is also pretty bad."

"So, I need to see what I am going to see and get back here before the alarm goes off?" Angela replied. "How long will I have?"

"Given the time those guys are supposed to go in there?" Hina explained. "You will have fifteen minutes to get in there ... ten minutes in there and fifteen back ... so thirty-five total? Do you think you can do that?"

"I have done more with less time while wearing a space suit," Angela said with a grin. "This is definitely doable!"

The timing had to be perfect and Angela went over the route and the timing several times before heading in. With the VIP's from the Bilderberg group still in the facility it was easy to get around unnoticed. The meeting accidentally proved to be a greater distraction than anything she could have hoped for. She got into a maintenance room, opened the vent and climbed inside. It was a tight fit with Angela's broad shoulders but she was able to move carefully and start making progress. Angela could not help but think of the scene from "Aliens" where Bishop, the android, crawled through the tight tunnel to get to the remote to call the drop ship. As Angela crawled, strange ideas came to her in the diminished light. She had always enjoyed movies with aliens in them, even from a young age. How could she watch any of them ever again after she had seen an alien craft and deciphered an extra-terrestrial code? Angela laughed to herself despite the stress and worry. It was a strange thought for a weird moment.

Angela had gloves on so she did not leave any fingerprints on the surface. She was practically invisible now but could not afford to leave anything behind. She wore a watch to keep a close eye on the time and was making great progress. By the time she got to the vent in the supposed area, she was four minutes ahead of schedule. She looked out from the vent and saw a small room with a simple chair. She had thought that maybe she was in the wrong place, expecting some sort of strange or sinister chamber or device.

Angela's doubts were put to rest as Enrick arrived with an unfamiliar man she could only presume was one of the people who had been volunteered the day before. The man was told to sit in the chair and he obediently did so. Angela watched. Confused as to what was going on.

"Does it hurt at all?" the man asked, seeming like he had grown nervous.

"Somewhat," Enrick replied. "But you must understand it and more is worth it for what you are about to become. You will cease to be who you are and become an amalgam. You will be immortal and perfected."

"Will I keep my mind?" the man asked. "Will I still be me?"

"Of course, you will," Enrick said with a smile. "You will just be much, much more."

Angela felt her heart racing as she waited to see what would happen. There seemed to be nothing in the room, nothing that would indicate something strange was about to occur. Enrick simply reached into his coat pocket and produced a strange device. It looked like a jury-rigged computer board with some manner of drive attached to it. He reached up and the device to the mans head. Instantly the subject started to scream, his body twitching like he was trying to move but couldn't. His eyes began to glow and he began to drool. Suddenly Enrich removed the device and the glowing stopped.

"Welcome," Enrick replied. "You have come a long way."

"Thank you," the man replied, his voice sounding slightly different, now devoid of emotion. "I have long anticipated coming here. I have this subjects memories ... I will be able to pass as him soon enough."

"He asked if he would still be him," Enrick replied. "I told him he would be."

"Cruel," the man responded with a slight smile. "Are all humans so gullible?"

"Not all," Enrick replied. "Many are self centred, paranoid, and quick to judge."

"Something we will cure them of," the man replied. "Well worth the effort as well I am told. Is it true how fast they breed?"

"It is unbelievable," Enrick replied. "In the years I have been here, I have personally seen nine of them become with child. They seem to be in some kind of rush to overpopulate this planet."

"Well that is the reason we are here, is it not?" the man replied. "A vast seemingly inexhaustible supply of hosts?"

"Indeed," Enrick replied. "Soon Nemesis will be in range and we won't have to use the signal to send our consciousness's here ... we can do it on a full scale."

"Do they have any idea what is coming?" the man asked. "Do they have the scientific means to track us?"

"They are on the verge of it," Enrick said. "Though I have personally gone to great lengths to suppress it."

"Well let us get our associate," the man said as he stood from his chair. He stared at his hands as if he was seeing them for the first time. "We can discuss the details later. Will the next subject ask if he will be him afterwards?"

"I can almost guarantee he will," Enrich replied. "Though they want immortality here so bad they will risk anything."

"Such silly things these creatures," the man replied. "If only they knew the true cost of immortality."

Angela wanted to watch more, wanted to know everything but she realized she was running out of time. She knew she got there fast but would have to go through a longer route to get turned around. She was already cutting it too close in waiting as long as she did. She forced her way back, leaving the strange sight behind her. As she went, time ticked away. Turning around took longer than she had thought and she assumed she could shave the same time off on the way back. By the time she got back to the maintenance room, got out, and replaced the cover she had only half a minute left. She walked out, moving as fast as she could but not at a run. She knew that she probably might be OK if she got stranded out here but her being in the office with Hina was her best cover. She moved quickly, calming her breaths as she went and slid into the office. Just as the door closed the alarm went off.

"You really cut that close!" Hina said in relief. "Did you make it in?"

Angela sat down, her head spinning. What she had heard was almost too much to process. It seemed unbelievable but she was there. She saw it with her own eyes. All the pieces fit and it was much more terrifying than she ever could have imagined. "I ... saw ... a lot."

"Angela you're scaring me," Hina replied. "How bad was it?"

"Bad," Angela replied. "I had my suspicions before, but it is much deeper. We need more help. We need to get everyone together and figure this out."

"Well we are supposed to go out on mission, right?" Hina replied. "I don't know how comfortable I am in here anymore."

"Well I think I have learned all I can here," Angela agreed. "We still play along but we must reunite with the others. There are people who want to fight what is coming ... we just need to figure out how."

"I agree," Hina nodded. "I am with you no matter what. I was naive to think that none of this stuff mattered. I used to think it was like a game. I can't go back to thinking like that ... I refuse."

"I'm happy to have you on my side," Angela said with a smile. "We need to stay together."

"How close are they?" Hina asked. "When will the aliens come?"

Angela sighed. "They are already here ... and have been so for some time."

CHAPTER FOUR
On the Outside looking in.

After the meeting of the Bilderberg group, Angela and Hina were given some free reign over their next assignments. They simply listed that they were going to search out and attempt to infiltrate the Second Sun organization and that was enough to get the green light. They were careful to check to make sure they were not monitored or followed but it seemed they finally had earned the trust of the brass at NASA. Hina and Angela now were now the people who would do the tracking so they were now safe to move on their own. Hina had been working for NASA for quite some time and did not really have her own place. Angela decided that she was already committed to this and her home would be as good a place as any. She took Hina to her downtown apartment, sweeping for bugs first before settling in.

"You live here?" Hina asked, looking around and marvelling at the apartment.

"Yeah. It used to be my parents place and when they passed, it came to me," Angela explained. "It is much more space than I need but I suppose if we are going to set up shop we are going to need it."

"Are there more?" Hina asked. "More than just you and me?"

Almost as if to answer, there was a knock at the door. Angela moved over, checking the peephole before the opened the door. She smiled to Hina as she opened it to reveal a young man and an older professor looking gentleman.

"Hina, may I introduce my other conspirators …" Angela said, gesturing to her friends. "Octan and Professor Gormanski."

"Pleased to meet you," Hina said with a nod. "I am Hina."

Octan blushed as he smiled at Hina, "Angela tells me you are a computer engineer?"

"I am," Hina smiled. "Are you the hacker that helped her track the southern array?"

"Plenty of time to get to now each other soon enough," Angela replied, ushering everyone in and closing the door. "For now, I've got to get everyone up to speed."

The group came in and set up in the large living room. Angel had kept a lot of what she knew and said to herself that the others seemed excited to find out what was going on. She stood up in front of her small band of information-seeking misfits and cleared her throat.

"My time in the inner workings of NASA were both hectic and worthwhile. I found out a lot but also had to become what we are fighting against … in a sense."

"What do you mean?" Gormanski asked. "You didn't kill anyone, did you?"

"No," Angela replied as she looked on to Hina. "I am not saying my hands are clean, but I did not do that nor was I asked to. The worst was that I kind of destroyed BriarTech."

"That was NASA?" Octan asked in shock. "That is, like one of the most efficient corporate smears of all time."

"It was my big test for NASA," Angela replied. "But that is just the tip of the iceberg."

"Did you find evidence?" Gormanski asked. "Are they in conflict with aliens?"

"They are the aliens," Angela replied. "At least now they are. It seems it is much deeper than we thought. The aliens seem to have the ability to possess human bodies and have replaced NASA head officials and other key members. There was a meeting of an organization known as the Bilderberg group and as I watched they replaced the minds of one of their members. There could be aliens in key places in the power centers of the worlds governments."

"How do we combat such a thing?" Octan asked. "They could be anyone … they could be one of us."

"We should first try to find a way to detect one of them," Hina added. "If we can't tell who is a human and who is an alien, we can't really do much against them."

"Agreed," Angela admitted. "That is definitely a good way forward.

We need to think of anything that might be able to detect a human with an alien mind within them."

"What about the signal?" Gormanski added. "Did you figure out what that was about?"

"Not precisely," Angela admitted. "We kind of got off on the top floor with what we uncovered and witnessed. They referred to something called 'Nemesis' and that it is coming. When it is here they will not have to take us over from a distance."

"Actually, that gives me an idea about the signal," Gormanski explained as he pulled out a notepad and began to draw. "This is their planet and this is earth. The signal is much more complex than we know and all we know is the basics of how it works. It is reasonable that with the right receptor that they can receive something big through it … such as an alien consciousness."

"They had something like that," Angela commented. "Enrick has some kind of device he put to the head of one of the people he possessed."

"That makes sense!" Gormanski added. "It would be dangerous to broadcast something such as a consciousness just over the open wave. There's no counting for who it could go into or if it made it at all. The device likely tells the other end to send and when it does, it receives it."

"What about nemesis though?" Hina added. "We don't know what that is."

"Well I have a theory for that," Octan added as he took the diagram from Gormanski. They are using this signal to mimic the gravitational co-ordinates of the Earth. As we discussed, this is an amazing breakthrough but it has its limits. It is like a radio signal … it can only go so far, stifled by the curvature of the earth. However, a satellite can send the signal even further. Now, also keep in mind the satellite is limited to what it can send and how fast based on it's position. What if this signal, which is cheating space time by using gravity was very weak when it started. It was barely hitting the earth and only the highest up … like NASA heard it. Now there's no way of us knowing how the first alien got through, but somehow, they took over NASA. The fact that they seem to be doing one or two at a time means they can't do them all the time. They need to wait until whatever this Nemesis is to get even closer to do more and more sending."

"Well that is consistent with some theories on Nemesis," Gormanski added.

"There actually is a Nemesis?" Angela asked.

"Not exactly," Gormanski replied. "It is technically an absence of a thing. There are certain … gravitational anomalies in our solar system that would suggest that there is something that comes through our galaxy on a returning orbit."

"Like another planet?" Octan asked.

"More likely another star," Gormanski replied.

"That's strange," Angela commented, fitting the pieces together in her mind. "NASA is VERY protective over an idea of a second sun … so much that the people who are opposing NASA have named their secret organization after it."

"I have been hearing about this second sun," Octan added as he took out his laptop. "They have a decent presence on the deep web. They were very hard to find at first, but if you know where to look, you find them. They are there."

"I found one from a message board though his user habits," Hina bragged. "Such as his language structure and media quotes."

"There are algorithms that I hear could back trace almost any user through that," Octan replied. "But I have never seen one used before."

"I wrote it," Hina replied with a coy smile. "And they do work."

"I think we need to get back on topic kids," Gormanski scolded.

"So, there is a theory of a second sun that might exist in our known galaxy?' Angel asked. "Would that not be easy to see?"

"Yes and no," Gormanski explained. "We know of it's existence because of … anomalies in the orbits of the planets in our solar system. It all started when an astrophysicist tried to find a solution to these numbers not adding up. When you need to solve a problem, when you can't see the affecting factors, you need to try theorizing and see what fits. When he plotted what would happen if it were another orbit from a long distant star, the equation filled in and worked the way it was supposed to. From the length of the axis and the gravitational forces needed, he surmised it would have to be a star or something like it. Keep in mind that this orbit could take thousands or hundreds of thousands of years. It is so long that the last time it likely came within viewing distance, there was not intelligent life to look up and see it."

"Could this be the alien's planet somehow?" Octan asked. "Could they be planning to invade from it?"

"Not from a star," Gormanski said with a perked eyebrow. "Even if they are in fact pure energy it is unlikely they could survive the forces of such a place. The fact that they can takeover human bodies shows that they at least have a familiarity with flesh and blood hosts. Speaking from our knowledge of evolution, that is not just something you develop. They either are leaving their biological bodies behind or they jump from body to body. I cannot see how they could survive without them. However, keep in mind this is all theoretical … no one has a lot of experience on this type of life form … at least not in this solar system."

"The sun generates a lot of gravitational forces, right?" Angela asked.

"An almost indescribable amount," Gormanski confirmed. "What are you thinking?"

"What if it is an amplifier of some sort?" Angela theorized. "The gravitational wave that is connecting their world to ours is being sent around the gravitational forces of this nemesis star and then sending it to our sun then to earth."

"That is theoretically possible," Gormanski commented. "There is not any kind of technology to do that here, but were they able to do it that would be a very efficient way to send complex signals indeed."

"Well, they said Nemesis was coming," Angela replied. "And since they were currently on Earth at the time, they meant it was coming here. Now even giving how fast stars and orbital bodies move soon is kind of a strange thing to say. "

"Yeah like from it being too far to detect to being close enough to affect us is a long, long time," Octan added. "Like hundreds of years. Earth would literally see something like that coming … like with telescopes and civilian technology. There's no way they could hide it's coming."

Angela sighed, "Even though they said soon, we have no way to gauge when it will be close enough to worry about. We need to find out how to determine how much time we have left."

"I would surmise that by here, it is as relatively close as it is going to get in ours and their lifetimes," Gormanski theorized. "So, by here they are expressively referring to the fact that it becomes close enough to affect their plans in a significant way. Since the star would not change speed, they must mean that some manner of deferring factor will no longer affect it. Like an asteroid field or obstruction that deters a significant part of the signal passes."

"That makes much more sense, but we still need to figure out what it is," Angela explained as she looked over her small group. "The fact that NASA is so paranoid about the Second Sun might be because they know more about this star and it's coming than anyone else. I think we need to think like our enemy and seek out their enemy. We need to find and infiltrate the Second Sun and get their information and pair it with ours."

"That will not be easy," Gormanski replied. "These are some of the most secretive and paranoid people on earth."

"Well, so are we," Angela grinned. "Octan and Hina will hit the deep web and try to unravel as much of their network as they can."

"On it," Hina said with a grin … Octan smiling as well but Angela suspected for a different reason.

"I want you to check all your contacts," Angela said to Gormanski. "You are somewhat of a celebrity in the conspiracy world and you might uncover something we can use."

"You realise that NASA will be all over me the second I enquire about the Second Sun, right?" Gormanski asked.

"No, they won't," Angela replied. "I am going to inform them exactly what we are doing. As of right now, what we are searching for is in their best interests. I will tell them we are using you for contacts. You are going to have a lot more freedom on the web than you've had in years."

"This is where I'd normally tell you how crazy that is," Gormanski replied. "Though this is actually genius."

"We are in a rare period where our work coincides with NASA's agenda," Angela explained. "They want the second sun organization found as badly as we do. We just have to make sure that we find the right time to split off … the time where the agendas polarize."

Everyone agreed and started to get to work. They had no more leads and information then they usually did but the direction forward motivated them all to work at it as hard as they could.

***

The apartment went from being a rarely lived in space to the head-quarters of something bigger. Since they were working for NASA's benefit, there was less need for secrecy, and it actually benefited the group to know that they were listening. Angela would update Stone and found not only was he okay with the developing situation, he was quite excited. Gormanski and Octan, of course, were working for NASA under different names and were just listed as private contracted analysts … something that NASA had no issue with Angela bringing on. There were, of course, rules put in place by Angela for what could be said to NASA and what could not. As long as they delivered something, the other side seemed uninterested in hearing the rest.

NASA was known for their huge budget, especially for their cloak and dagger projects, which, by definition, are off books. With the field work came access to these funds and Angela decided that it be fitting to use it for this. Her apartment was now outfitted with several cutting-edge computers and just about every tool Hina and Octan could dream of. Angela toured her new impromptu facility and admired how hard her friends were working.

"Do we have anything?" Angela asked, looking around to each person.

"I have had a few people reach out to me," Gormanski replied, looking up from his laptop. "I think most are crackpots, but some seem to have knowledge that they shouldn't. I forwarded it all for review."

"I am scouring the deep web for anything similar to the new information," Octan explained. "I am not sifting through it, just archiving it."

"That is where I come in," Hina bragged. "I am just putting it all together and running it through an algorithm that looks for connections and tries to suggest patterns. One or two of these users or comments might seem unrelated but if they connect with enough together, they paint a picture of the bigger network."

"That makes a lot of sense," Angela replied. "These Second Sun people cover their tracks well, relying like we did, that they did not leave a trail of breadcrumbs behind them for us to follow."

"This usually works well," Octan replied. "For if you can't find the pieces, you can't figure out what they were trying to do."

"However, we know better," Hina added. "We just ignore trying to find out anything at first and just assemble the crumbs wherever they are. We are essentially reforming the bread and from there we will know everything."

"Imagine what they would have been able to accomplish should they have skipped time coming up with that analogy," Gormanski joked.

"It will work!" Hina replied. "And I have discovered that if I tell people the technical explanations of what I do, their eyes glaze over."

"I hate that!" Octan added. "I get that a lot."

"Okay kids, enough bonding," Gormanski added. "We have a lot of work to do."

"This is weird," Octan commented suddenly. "Here it is again."

"Again?" Angel asked, moving over to Octan. "What is it?"

"A strange phrase," Octan replied. "It has been popping up a lot on the boards I have been searching."

"What is the phrase?" Angela asked. "Is it relevant to any of our searches?"

"It isn't really relevant to anything," Octan admitted. "It reads *A Lone Layman Signal.*"

"A lone layman signal?" Angela asked, searching her mind for anything familiar about it. "That means nothing to me … does it mean anything to anyone else?"

The group looked at each other, but no one had anything.

"How is it used?" Angela asked. "What is the context?"

"There is none," Octan replied. "It just pops up like that. Like I just got it on a thread about malfunctioning satellites and fifth response down is just a lone layman signal. Another one about missing people it pops up on the second page."

"Is it a single username?" Angela asked. "Can we use Hina's algorithm to find out who posted it?"

"A different username each time," Hina added. "The person posting it has gone to great lengths to make the usernames and login information untraceable."

"How many times has this phrase shown up?" Angela asked. "Could it be multiple people … some sort of prank or spam."

"As of now, I have come across close to thirty postings," Octan replied. "I could search it to find more."

"It is likely only one person," Hina explained. "The more people who take part in a posting war like this, the easier it is to track. I'd bet this is a single user."

Angela thought to herself, though the phrase was mostly nonsense, something in her gut told her it was somehow significant. "Can you search for every use of this phrase?"

"Of course," Octan replied. "It is a rather unique assortment of words. I can do both the deep web and surface net."

"You think this phrase means something?" Gormanski asked. "It sounds like nonsense to me."

"I don't know," Angela replied. "Though, if I have learned anything in all, it's that you need to pick the extraordinary from the ordinary. This is just too weird to ignore."

"Hey, I think I might have something here," Hina broke in. "I was cataloguing the contacts from Gormanski and a name popped up."

"Popped up how?" Angela asked. "Like in a pattern."

"I mean like popped up on the news," Hina corrected. "I have my Facebook open and this guys name just came up on my feed."

"Who is it?" Angela asked as she came over to Hina to see her screen.

"A guy by the name of Harold Cozy," Hina replied. "He is a programming genius … made that game *Mermaids Kiss*."

"I've known him forever," Gormanski commented. "Even before he was a billionaire."

"Well, he is doing some sort of talk," Hina replied. "Really mysterious and urgent. His shareholders are concerned and he won't reveal what it is about. However, he has not only told the press, he has hired people to film what he is about to say and got broadcasting time for it on major networks."

"Do you think it is related to what we are doing?" Octan asked. "It could be just a coincidence."

"It could be just a coincidence is a famous phrase for those who missed seeing a pattern," Gormanski explained. "Cozy is more paranoid than I am and hates public speaking. This is really strange … even for him."

"When is it?" Angela asked. "How close."

"About an hour and in the city," Hina replied. "I forwarded you the information."

"I'm going to check it out," Angela said as she got ready to leave. "Everyone keep at it … worst case this is a waste of time … best case something big will happen."

Within the hour, Angela was in the courtyard to the office building Cozy ran his business out of. There was already a sea of reporters and curious parties gathered at the impromptu stage. Angela had the usual feeling of something out of the ordinary, but admitted to herself it was been a while since she had not felt it. She maneuvered through the crowd and took up a good spot to the side of the stage. She checked in with the others on her phone, but there was nothing other than an inquiry about ordering lunch.

The crowd grew louder and pushed in on itself as someone walked onto the stage. The man that Angela presumed was Cozy walked along the stage, looking like a man with purpose. Flashes went off and people began to shout questions but the man simply silenced them with a raised arm as he walked up to a microphoned podium.

"Thank you all for coming," Cozy began. "I am sorry to have called this with such urgency, but there is an issue that I have to get out into the open."

Angela felt her phone go off as in someone was calling her. She ignored it and let it go to voice mail.

"I know all of you are expecting news of my next game," Cozy continued. "Though that is definitely still in the works, this is about something else. As you know I have been branching out …"

Angela's phone went off again immediately and she put it to her ear. "Hello?"

"You have amazing instincts," Stone said over the phone. "You thought this was probably something to do with … our interests."

"Uh yeah," Angela said, looking around to see how she was spotted here by Stone while trying to focus on Cozy talking something about his ideals about humanity looking to space to avoid climate change. "Seemed kind of strange to me."

"Well you don't need to worry about it," Stone said simply. "We've got it taken care of."

"Taken care of?" Angela asked. "I don't understand."

"Pardon the commotion," Stone replied. "Keep a hold of your phone."

Angela looked confused as she looked back to Cozy who was continuing his speech, "I have been looking to the stars for too long and discovered that it is here where the problem lies. I have recently uncovered treachery here. Certain government officials have been lying to us and through …"

A gunshot went off, interrupting Coz's words. It was so sudden that

Angela could not even tell where he was hit. There were screams as the man was alive one moment and dead the next, simply slumping down next to the podium. The crowd surged around in a chaotic maelstrom, some instinctively trying to flee, some trying to move closer. Angela indeed almost dropped her phone as she was shoved. She focused on her task, trying to get into the sidelines and out of the impromptu mosh pit. She saw the attendees close to Cozy running over to help, but it was far too late.

Angela got to safety and looked back at her phone, "Was that you … us?"

"Of course it was," Stone replied. "That is why I said to be careful."

"What did he know?" Angela asked. "What made him such a target?"

"He got some proof that things were covered up," Stone replied. "Clever guy was spying on users through his games and apps. He was about to expose us, but we got a leak of his intended speech. By shooting him when we did, we can play it like he was about to call out a senator for corruption. No one will know or believe he was really after us."

"That is very cleaver," Angela praised, though still forcing herself to compartmentalise the horror of what she had seen and heard. "I guess that ties up that loose end. How did you know I was here? More surveillance?"

"Ho no," Stone replied. "We trust you. I just happened to be by the hotdog cart you walked by on the way in. Figured you deserved a heads up."

"Appreciated," Angela replied, still transfixed by the mayhem in front of her as emergency personal tried to make their way to Cozy, like it would make any difference. "I hope to … have some information for you soon."

"Good, good," Stone replied. "I really am looking forward to see what you come up with. We have been very impressed with your work thus far."

"I look forward to impressing you further," Angela lied. "I will contact you when I can."

Angela hung up the phone and started to make her way away from the chaos. She was no further to more answers but just got a grim reminder of the corrupt NASA's bag of tricks and the lengths they would go through for the protection of their secrets.

***

The next few days were mostly uneventful and Angela realized she was becoming desensitized to people being shot in front of her. She debated if that was a good thing or not but ultimately realized that it was an unfortunate par to the course of her recent life. She had told herself long ago that she had to get her hands dirty if she were to stop the people with the dirtiest hands. She went to her group to check on developments.

"I have been tracking the strange phrase," Octan began. "It has since popped up twenty-seven more times and it is looking more and more like something significant."

"Have we had any luck determining what it means?" Angela asked. "Is it some sort of code?"

"It is gibberish," Gormanski admitted. "It means literally nothing."

"What about a pattern?" Angela asked. "Does it show anything to the poster?"

"Yes and no," Hina added. "It is hard to explain. They are on a lot of treads and places and there seems to be part of a pattern. We just don't have enough of it."

"Either we have not found enough of them or whoever is doing them hasn't done enough," Octan replied. "I am still finding them but it seems like everything we find takes us a little closer to discovering it's meaning."

Angela crossed her arms, "I think this is definitely significant. If not, I still want to know what it means. It is eating me up inside."

"It might turn out to be some sort of prank," Gormanski added. "It could mean nothing at all."

"Either way we can't afford not to look at leads," Angela replied. "Anything on Second Sun?"

"That we do have traction on," Gormanski said, looking like he was excited to explain what was found. "We have not gotten many names yet but we are confident that they meet here … in Washington. They apparently are meeting with an astronaut that has seen something."

"Yuri …" Angela guessed, realising she had not thought back to one of the first people to confirm her suspicions.

"You know him?" Gormanski asked. "Of the most credible reports of the signal from space, he seems to be the most credible."

"We went into space together," Angela asked. "Were it not for him, I might have opened my mouth a lot more than I did at the beginning."

"Well, it's good you didn't," Gormanski replied. "Were it not for him being very secretive, NASA would already be all over him."

"He was not easy to find," Octan admitted. "Took both me and Hina to smoke him out."

"I suppose we have become quite the team," Angela admitted. "So how does he connect to Second Sun."

"Well, once we identified Yuri, it was no hard matter to track what he was doing," Hina explained. "He apparently has a picture of the thing in space … an unedited one … and he wants to share it with someone that won't suppress it. The Second Sun wants it and they are going to do a meeting."

"Where?" Angela said, growing suddenly determined. She didn't just want answers, she wanted to protect Yuri.

"You will need to be careful," Gormanski added. "He is threatening showing up in NASA's crosshairs and the Second Sun are going to be very skittish should you try to get in on this."

"The only way to protect him might be to recruit him," Angela explained. "Also, the Second Sun was asking for one astronaut who has seen the disturbance … they will love getting two."

Two days later Angela waited in a coffee shop a mere five blocks from her apartment. She was no stranger to such clandestine meetings as this is exactly how her little band had started. She looked around at the individuals in the shop, having no real way of knowing if the Second

Sun members were in fact already there. She kept her eyes out for Yuri, hoping to catch him as he came in. This might endanger his chances of the Second Sun revealing themselves but she knew if she tried to break in after they met they would never trust her.

Moments later Yuri entered. He looked just as spooked as he had last time she saw him. The pair locked eyes immediately and he came to sit down.

"What are you doing here?" Yuri asked urgently.

"Long story but I know why you are here and I am here to help," Angela replied. "I have gone down the rabbit hole and come back out, so I am going to have to ask you to trust me."

Yuri looked around for a moment, "I suppose in the sea of people I don't trust that I am swimming in you are the most trustworthy person I know."

"Good," Angela replied. "I need to meet with the Second Sun and need you to vouch for me."

"Vouch for you?" Yuri asked. "These guys make it their business to be secretive."

"So do I," Angela explained. "After all this, I want to know you what I have been up to."

"Fair enough," Yuri replied. "I am supposed to text my contact for when he comes in. I will tell him I have another witness with me."

"Thank you," Angela replied. "This will work out for both of us. I can protect us both, I swear."

Yuri send the text and within moments two men entered the coffee shop. They walked right to the table and sat down, no introductions or excuses offered.

"I understand you both have seen it," one of the men asked … he had a thick beard and thicker glasses.

"We have," Yuri answered. "On more than one occasion."

"Do you know what it is?" another of the men asked, this one with a dark bowl haircut.

"It is some manner of transmitter," Angela replied. "That much I am sure."

"Really?" the dark-haired man responded. "That is very astute of you."

"We also know what the transmission is for and what it does," Angela replied.

Yuri looked at Angela surprised, seeming to be confirmed in that she knew what she was talking about. "My associate has done her own research. We have a lot of proof."

"What is it you are hoping to do with it?" the bearded man asked. "We can pay for verifiable information."

"More so, we are looking for allies," Angela replied. "There is a lot going on and we want to do our best to fight against the corruption … before it is too late."

"That is kind of not how we operate," the bearded man admitted. "We are not secret agents or anything like that."

"What do you mean?" Yuri said as he leaned in. "You guys are NASA'S public enemy number one and you do not want to fight back against what they are doing?"

"Well, we worked hard to get that level of notoriety," the dark-haired man replied. "Though, it is not to fight them. Do you have any idea the amount of money that NASA is working with?"

"This is about extortion?" Yuri asked in an annoyed tone. "You want the proof of what they are doing so you can milk NASA of money to keep it silent."

"It is not easy," the bearded man admitted. "But it is a pretty lucrative operation. You get to be in on it. We are willing to pay top dollar … via untraceable bitcoin no less for what you know and can give us."

Angela could see anger building up in Yuri, the usual boisterous Russian clearly not liking his risks and challenges being reduced to a dollar figure when all he wanted was validation and allies. She suspected he was about to lose it on the men.

"Figured as much," Angela replied. "Yuri, I think we should make a deal."

"You do?" Yuri asked in obvious surprise.

"Yeah," Angela said in surprise. "What can we possibly do against such a giant. I suppose we might as well profit from it. As long as they have insurances of our names not being on record."

"I suppose I am alright with that," Yuri said as he took a memory card out and put it on the table. "This is the original memory card with the photos I took. They are unaltered and with the camera data still on it."

"Good, good," the black-haired man said as he put the card in a small portable device. "Damn this is good."

"The funds will be transferred to an account and you will be contacted on how to access it," the bearded man explained as he and his associate stood up. "A pleasure doing business with you."

After the pair left, Yuri turned to Angela with a confused look on his face, "What the hell just happened? I thought they were like us … seekers of the truth?"

"They still sought it," Angela admitted. "But for their own gains. I can't believe NASA wants them so badly and all they are just opportunists and extortionists."

"Where do you fit into all of this?" Yuri asked.

"Well, I started out like you," Angela began. "Someone who wanted answers. However, I decided to go a bit deeper. Full disclosure, I am a double agent with NASA and am helping them search for people against them, at the same time cataloguing their movements. We have discovered some frightening things and want to see what we can do to stop it. You can just walk away if you want, but if you are with me, you come into the belly of the beast."

"To take it down from the inside?" Yuri asked. "I don't know why I never thought of that."

"It is dangerous and I am taking a risk telling you what I did," Angela admitted. "And I would ask the same risk of you."

"I'm in," Yuri said with a nod. "But I am still upset the Second Sun turned out to be so slimy."

"Oh, don't worry so much about that," Angela said with a smile. "I already have a plan for them."

"Do tell?" Yuri asked. "Because I just gave them the smoking gun and I really don't feel good about it."

"Well, they have exactly what NASA fears they will get," Angela explained. "I am going to call my handler at NASA and tell them I recruited you. I also am going to sell those Second Sun assholes so far up the river that they won't know what hit them. With that NASA, will give us greater freedom and resources and we will have unprecedented access to their secrets."

"That's amazing!" Yuri admitted. "I'm in. But how will you get them. They are very well protected and we don't even know their names."

"Oh, they are," Angela smiled as she put her phone on the table. "But my phone was rigged to interface with theirs within a proximity. Everything on their phones is ours now. I once challenged a college friend of mine to do this and she finally got it working."

"You are really scary sometimes, you know that?" Yuri said with a smile. "But I think we need someone like you if were going to figure out how to fight back."

"You have no idea," Angela replied. "But we are going to fight back … that much I promise you."

***

All it took was one call to Stone and the forwarding of the Second Suns information from the phone and the hounds went out. Within an hour, any sign of the Second Sun on the deep web was gone and it was like they never existed. Angela was glad to have Yuri on board. She admitted that she was worried about him back when this whole thing first started and felt guilty for not reaching out to him before this. However, as she brought him before her motley crew of hackers and conspiracy experts, it seems that he had finally found what he was looking for.

"I am very pleased to meet you all," Yuri said with a polite nod. "I am glad to find people that are actually working toward exposing the truth … the others proved to me … less than reliable."

"Very nice to meet you as well," Gormanski nodded. "I had been following your leaks since day one."

Angela smiled to Yuri, "Right now, we are not exposing NASA because we discovered that there was a lot of information that only they had. Did you read the brief that I gave you?"

"Yeah," Yuri admitted. "Strange symbols, downloadable aliens. It is all stuff that would sound ludicrous had it not somehow all fit together."

"Many times, I have found myself wishing it was too strange to be true," Octan interjected. "It is like a bad episode of the x-files, but, unfortunately, it is very true. NASA relies though on the fact that any one piece of this without the corresponding evidence seems like the ravings of a lunatic."

"Well I believe in it," Yuri said with a nod. "I have seen the ship myself."

"That reminds me," Gormanski added. "With all our research on a broadcasted signal and the two suns … what exactly is that thing you saw in space?"

"To be honest I am not quite sure," Angela admitted. "With everything that we have discovered and everything we searched for, the answer to the thing starting it all eludes us. What is that thing and what does it do? It obviously had something to do with the signal, but what?"

"Well it is an anomaly to what we know about the situation," Gormanski admitted. "In approaching any situation such as this we need the who, what, when, why, and how. The *who* … that's simple … it is NASA and aliens that have taken over bodies and the entire upper infrastructure of the organization. The *what* is a conspiracy to cover up the alien's conquest of earth. The *why* is because they need our bodies and the *how* is with that device and broadcasting from sun to sun with gravitational co-ordinate wavelengths."

"But we don't have the *when*," Angela added. "We don't know when these aliens got here and when they took over NASA."

"Exactly," Gormanski replied. "We have no idea how they originally found us on earth or how they took over."

"It's like the chicken and the egg," Octan added. "What came first ... a possessed person or the alien to possess him?"

"Why is all this necessary?" Yuri asked. "Do we not have a plan on what we are to do against NASA?"

"Not yet," Gormanski admitted. "We are still figuring things out."

Yuri seemed to grow more and more frustrated, "Well, while we are figuring things out as you say, the aliens further their agenda and move closer and closer to a time where no one will be able to stop them. The time for action is upon us ... if it isn't already too late."

"Well, we don't know how yet," Angela said, trying to reassure her friend. "They have built an empire of secrets and have become very good at dealing with leaks and whistleblowers. Even now, if we went to every press agency that would listen and reported to all manners of committees and law enforcement, it would only cause another conspiracy storm. Even if we hurt them, it would cause so much chaos that it could take YEARS for it to get sorted out and all the while they would be able to further their plans behind the scenes."

"We need to find a way to fight them," Yuri insisted. "What good is this information if we are all replaced by aliens?"

"If we go off before we are ready, we doom ourselves to fail," Angela replied. "We need all the answers, we need to identify a weakness."

"What if they don't have a weakness?" Yuri retorted? "Are we just going to wait forever looking for one?"

"I need to interject," Hina spoke up, looking up from her laptop for the first time since the discussion began.

"Not now Hina," Angela replied, still looking at Yuri and trying to think of a way to convince him to her course of action.

"Actually, this is important!" Hina insisted. "It kind of can't wait."

Angela sighed and turned to Hina, "I'm sorry. What is it?"

"I have a lead on the strange postings," Hina began. "Well not so much of a lead, but a development."

"What kind of development?" Angela asked.

"Well, the person stopped posting," Hina replied.

"How could we know they are done?" Octan asked. "They could be just taking a break."

"No, they are done," Hina reaffirmed. "The posts are all part of a message and when I fed them into the computer they spelled it out. Each post by it self seems random and innocent. However, the ways they are posted as well as how they are posted is a pattern. I had set the computer model to identify when the pattern made sense and it just did. This corresponded with a lapse in posting that is longer than any break since they started showing up. I know what they were trying to say with these posts."

"What is it?" Angela asked. "A message?"

"A place and time," Hina replied. "The pattern is a series of numbers. The first of which is a GPS co-ordinate and the second is a time."

"Where and when?" Angela asked.

"The co-ordinate seems to be an abandoned warehouse forty-five minutes from here and the when is tonight at one minute after twelve."

"You're not thinking of going, are you?" Gormanski asked. "This is the most bizarre invitation I have ever heard of."

"I don't know," Angela replied. "How likely is it that anyone else has gotten this?"

"Very unlikely," Hina replied. "The fact that we were looking so intently at it is the only reason we were able to figure it out. Only those on the deep web who were looking at what were searching for with our skillset could figure it out."

"It sounds like a trap to me," Gormanski insisted. "I don't like it."

"I don't know," Angela replied. "The sophistication and elaborate means behind this message is amazing. We need to know what it means. The phrase has bored into my mind and I need to figure it out."

"What phrase?" Yuri asked. "I don't understand."

"It's gibberish," Octan explained. "The whole thing started when we found a nonsense phrase posted again and again on the deep web. As far as we know there is no meaning to *A lone layman signal*."

"It's an anagram," Yuri replied.

"Wait, what?" Octan replied. "Are you sure?"

"Yes, I am sure," Yuri replied. "I used to do this all the time with my friends."

"How did we miss that?" Octan replied.

"It is so simple that you went right over it," Gormanski said with a laugh.

"It takes a long time to unscramble anagrams of that length," Hina replied. "I can program a ..."

"I think I got it," Yuri replied. "There aren't many real sentence's that fit this but this one does and I think it is it."

"Tell us," Angela asked. "What does the phrase say?"

"If you rearrange the letters of A Lone Layman signal ..." Yuri began. "You get *An ally among aliens*."

"Woah," Gormanski replied in an uncharacteristic moment of awe. "That is remarkable."

"They don't let just anyone be astronauts," Yuri said with a grin. "Most of us are pretty bright."

"Well assuming that anagram is correct, how does the poster mean it?" Octan asked. "Does he mean that he is among the aliens like we are? A person who is against the NASA secret agenda but is from the inside?"

"I think we need to find out one way or another," Angela suggested. "Yuri does have one point and that is that we need to start planning on how to fight back. We don't know their weaknesses and we do not know enough to make any sort of real dent in their plans. I have made most of my strides in what we are doing for being bold. So, I am going to go to this meeting."

"But what if it is a trap?" Gormanski addressed again. "It could be Second Sun people that escaped the witch hunt."

"Unlikely," Octan explained. "For this signal came from before we exposed them and they seemed to have no real desire to do anything beyond blackmail."

"Could be NASA then?" Gormanski theorized. "Trying to hunt out any trailers or moles."

"A little more likely, but I am pretty sure if NASA thought I was a mole they would have better ways to discover it," Angela replied. "This is above that sort of thing. I am not saying that it might not be a trap, but if someone was looking for allies in such a deep level, this might be the best way to find them. Look at it! They made a trail of breadcrumbs so hard to find that only people like themselves might be able to follow it. To be honest I am wondering why we did not try something like this to get allies of our own. Heck I think if this works out we should still do it."

"I am inclined to agree with you," Yuri said with a nod. "I went to the Second Sun because I did not want to be alone in this fight. They turned out to be frauds, but that does not mean that I still don't need allies. I am lucky to have found you all but we are still too few. If we are to take the fight to NASA we will need every able body we can get our hands on."

"Alright," Gormanski admitted. "We should check this out. But you should not go alone."

"I do not want to risk our entire group," Angela replied. "If this is a trap to smoke us out, I want to make sure that each of you has deniability with others and with NASA that I was not making you go to my agenda."

"Then let me go with you," Yuri replied. "I have not been part of this long and if I am caught as well it will not affect the rest."

"Agreed," Angela replied. "We will go to this meeting and hope for the best. I keep saying the answers are out there but for as many as I find, more become more hidden. This could be the big one, someone who knows the inner workings that could lead to our having a plan."

"Be safe," Octan added. "As much as I hate NASA's agenda, what I really care about is you."

"I know," Angela said with a smile. "This group is the endearing creation of all this darkness and the thing that reminds me to look away when I gave in too long at the abyss."

Yuri smiled, "No matter what happens, I want to thank you all for accepting me. There is still good left in this world of lies and secrets and I am glad to have seen some of it."

***

The co-ordinates listed lead Yuri and Angel far across town to a more industrial district. It was an area that was still being renovated and there were still a lot of uninhabited industrial complexes left behind by older business. Angela felt a sense of dramatic irony that the building in question seemed to be … until rather recently to be a BriarTech ware-house. This posed as a grim and immediate reminder of what was at stake and to show that even the mightiest of organizations can not be safe. Angela had thought to herself that this is the kind of thing that people usually come armed to. However, she did not own a gun beyond an old hunting rifle in a family cottage. She was no stranger to defend-ing herself but never was really one for violence. She decided that if this situation was a trap, her very appearance would mean bad things … gun or not. She also thought back to all the gun related deaths that had dotted her journey thus far and the last thing she wanted to see is another one.

Yuri, for his part seemed fairly calm but Angela could tell that he was feeling the same suspicion and cautious dread as she did. Going into space was as frightening as it was exhilarating and she knew all too well how he showed stress. This was potentially either a new beginning to the mission or it's end. Angela was getting better and better at taking such bold risks and she did not know if that was a good thing or not. She worried that she might grow too bold, thinking herself invincible and that might lead to a fall. Though with everything that was indeed at stake she had to think of the bigger picture and not worry so much about herself. The act of objective selflessness was powerful in a world of paranoia and conspiracy and it might be the main thing that had made her so successful. She also learned what she can endure to see and do as well as the things she was willing to do for what she thought was right.

The warehouse seemed abandoned but showed signs that was not exactly the case. It was well maintained and at some point, security probably patrolled it. However, on this night the gates were wide open, lights were mostly off but with enough left on to illuminate the path. Whoever had set this up wanted to make it as easy for their invitees to attend but not to make it too obvious. Angela and Yuri simply walked through the gate, not seeing a soul as they headed deeper inside. As they got to the front door of the facility, a massive horizontal garage style door, it automatically roared to life, opening for the pair to let them inside.

The building inside still had a lot of BriarTech stock. Angela marvelled on how quickly NASA had destroyed the company that they could not even liquidate stock. In the center of the building was a path, illuminated by selective lights that lead further and further into the place.

"This is where one of us should say something like *I don't like this*," Yuri commented. "Then the other person reminds them why they are here and it will likely be alright."

"Would it help if I reassured you like that?" Angela replied. "Because I better do it now as I am not so sure of things as we go."

"I suppose not," Yuri admitted. "Though we are here, I think it is probably too late to turn back."

"Much to late," Angela agreed, continuing to move forward.

At the center of the warehouse was a desk, set up at the edge of the light. A single figure sat in the chair, their identity and details obscured by how the light was set.

"Welcome," the shadowy figure said in a surprisingly polite tone. "Please come join me."

Angela nodded, seeing a pair of chairs in front of her. She took one and Yuri took the other.

"So, do we get to know who you are?" Angela asked, trying to stay confident and show her suspicion to the man.

"Ultimately any answer I would give you is meaningless," the figure replied. "The name Mr. Hurst will suffice."

"Do you know who we are?" Yuri asked.

"Of course, Yuri," Hurst replied. "I know who you both are but that is no matter. I will not be doing anything untoward with your information."

"We need some answers," Angela asked. "First, why did you summon us?"

"I will offer you all the answers you desire," Hurst replied. "For that is why we are all here, are we not? I have seen ... glimmers of your work online. You are very good at covering your tracks ... but not perfect. I did my best to make sure that none of it was noticed by anyone but me and decided that we needed to talk. Now this, of course, led to a problem. I had suspicions as to who you were but had no idea how to separate you from the other chafe ... the Second Sun for example. Such a pity they turned out to be like the boy band of conspiracies."

"Quite a disappointment," Yuri agreed.

"Indeed," Hurst continued. "Though I saw movements and techniques that were lightyears beyond most of NASA's analysts so I decided to send the message out. Only if you were as good as I suspected you were, would you crack it and come to me. Also, I am confident that no one else could do it so we have this rare opportunity to talk."

"What kind of answers can you offer us?" Angela asked. "And how do you know them? You are inside NASA's inner circle I presume."

"More so than you could imagine," Hurst replied. "I am privy to everything."

"How is that possible?" Angela asked. "They have been taken over by aliens. How could they possibly trust one of us so deeply?"

"An ally amongst aliens," Yuri quoted. "It is literal, isn't it? Meant to infer that there is an ally amongst the people who are aliens not just one in their midst."

"Very astute," Hurst replied. "Though this body is Jonathon Hurst, the mind inside is not from this solar system."

"You are an alien?" Angela asked, a feeling of dread pouring down her spine and her urge to leave floated up from below. "How could we possibly trust you?"

"Do you have any choice not to?" Hurst replied. "There are no military soldiers here? No NASA hitmen are coming and when you choose to you can just walk right out. However, I am here now and will answer anything."

"Why?" Angela asked, her suddenly most urgent of questions.

"Well, like humans we do not always share ideologies with each other," Hurst explained. "Our people do something which is fundamentally wrong and there are those among us … a soft-spoken minority, that want to put a stop to it."

"The harvesting of humans as hosts?" Angela asked.

"Precisely," Hurst replied. "My people are old, ancient beyond your people's ability to fully grasp. When a species is that old, evolution tends to abandon you. Every group of life forms has an end to their lifespan and eventually they either become something else or fade away into the stardust of the universe. However, my people preferred the former to the latter and made great strides to do so. If we could not save our fragile biological existences, we would find new ones. We learned to separate our consciousness's from our bodies and found hosts in another race upon our home world. There were millions of them but they were not enough. It was a scramble and many of our people were left to die, but when all was said and done, the other race was extinct as they were … all now hosts for us."

"I can't even picture this in my head," Yuri admitted. "It is just … surreal."

"It was so long ago I even have problems remembering what that species looked like," Hurst continued. "It proved a short-sighted solution as we proved to be detrimental to the other species. They could not breed while we inhabited them and soon the hosts were too frail to hold us. Our only solution was to find new hosts. We found a path through the stars, and using our great technology, went from inhabited planet to inhabited planet, trying to find lifeforms to sustain us. However, none were large enough to sustain us, so we went from host species to host species. We lost members of our own as we went but decimated entire peoples as we moved. We needed a fuller solution, something sustainable."

"Then you found us," Angela added. "Enrick commented interest in how fast we multiply."

"To us that is worth more than anything in the universe," Hurst explained. There are enough people on this world that all of us could take a host and still leave a significant amount to provide breeding stock for when those bodies fail. My people intend to turn this world to a body farm."

"That is terrifying," Yuri replied. "But … you don't want this?"

"No," Hurst replied. "I have lived hundreds of lifetimes and seen too much genocide and death. I wish for an end to this and there are others like me."

"Can you tell us how to stop them?" Angela asked.

"Yes and no," Hurst replied. "Though myself and others hold descent to the group, we can not work to actively harm them. We are all empathically connected in a way. We cannot read each others thoughts, but when extreme thoughts or emotions raise we can detect them. Should I tell you any deep information on how to hurt us, the others will potentially be able to know about it. You must understand that I can no more jeopardise my own conspirators in this than you can yours."

"Then what can you do?" Angela asked.

"Two things," Hurst replied. "I can actively supress any signs of what you are doing from being seen by the wrong people. Second is though I cannot tell you how to hurt us, I will answer any questions you have here. You may use that to figure out how to effectively fight us."

"What is in this for you?" Yuri replied. "Should we succeed, what do you want?"

"I do not profess to be above my own demands," Hurst replied. "I ask that only that myself and a companion of mine that are already in human form be allowed to live out our lives naturally and die as humans. That is assuming you are successful in stopping us."

"Is there any way to give humans their minds back?" Angela asked.

"Once they are taken?"

"No," Hurst replied without even trying to sugar-coat it. "The human brain is a complicated thing and we needed to remove all semblance of consciousness of the former users for it to work. I am sorry."

"The implications being what they are it is worth it to overlook it for the two of you for an ally," Angela replied. "We agree to your terms."

"Good," Hurst replied. "We do not have much time left but you may ask what you will. There will be … avenues for more questions but they will be more difficult later."

"Tell us how it started," Angela replied, thinking back to the questions from the earlier conversation at base. "How did you first get here?"

"That is a very good question," Hurst agreed. "For that we need to go to the beginning and I must show you things that might be too much for you."

"I can handle it," Angela insisted. "Tell me everything … I have come too far to be left with any more questions … now is the time for answers."

CHAPTER FIVE
The Returned Signal.

Angela found herself in a desert, she was surrounded by nothing for as far as the eye could see. She was confused, shaking her head.

"Where am I?" Angela said. "This makes no sense."

"Calm down Angela," the voice of Mr. Hurst broke in as he walked up beside her. "You are in my mind … so to speak."

"Wait, how?" Angela asked. "What are you doing to me?"

"Please remember," Hurst said in a simple tone. "I needed to show you things about the invasion and I offered to do so in your mind. You agreed to this."

As Angela slowly nodded her head, things starting to make sense like triggering real memories in a dream and then gaining control of it.

"Yes! Sorry, I remember."

"It is quite alright," Hurst replied. "It is hard for us to link with you in this way and it is not without its challenge."

Angela looked around, noticing that the landscape was far less alien than she expected.

"This is not your home world, is it?"

"No," Hurst replied. "It would be difficult for me to put the idea of what my … home looked like. Instead I am giving you the basic details and letting your brain populate it with things it knows."

"Ok that makes sense," Angela replied. "Ok, tell me what is going on."

Hurst nodded as he began to lead Angela through the desert.

"Think of this dessert as the vast reaches of space. You can imagine there are lots of things in it but they are so far apart it is difficult to tell the distance between things from ground level."

"Ok, that makes sense," Angela admitted, still at a bit of a loss but feeling like she understood it.

Hurst pointed. "Way down there is where we currently are … the place is in ruins and can no longer support us. This is like our planet. We know that there are countless planets out there and many with life that we might take. The issue is finding them."

Angela became aware of several vehicles, all starting from the area where Hurst pointed but all driving off in different directions.

"What are those?"

"Those are the scouts," Hurst explained. "In this analogy, they are supped up cars made to get the driver as far as possible. They are full of gas as well as communication equipment to call home. They only have the resources for a one-way trip and hopefully they can find something before they run out."

"They are launched into space with no hope of return?" Angela asked. "What if they find nothing?"

"Lost to space," Hurst replied. "It is a risk we take, a matter of numbers. Send out several and hope that one or two find something for the rest of us."

The setting shifted to a mad max style base, filled with people retrofitting cars and sending people out. In the center was a large array and people waiting to hear from it. Angela walked around, the figures paying her absolutely no heed.

"So, they just waited on your home world for some sign of life?"

"Millions," Hurst replied. "All waiting and sustaining their lives as long as they can."

Angela watched as a signal went off, and a tiny monitor showed earths solar system.

"One of your probes found earth?"

"Not exactly," Hurst admitted. "We sent several probes this way, hoping that there would be something. However, we found none. Almost all the probes went dark, but one made it, crashing on your moon. The one of us used the remaining power to survive as long as he could, thinking he failed. However, then one day a lander came and humans explored the barren surface."

"One of the lunar missions?" Angela asked.

"Indeed," Hurst replied as the scene shifted to a car broken down on the side of the road and a bus pulling up to help the stranded driver. "He was close to death but he managed to put himself in the body of your astronauts. He went back to earth with only the man's basic memories. He could not bring back any of his tech on the small lander and went back to your world with nothing. He spent years building himself up within NASA, eventually contacting the others and making it possible for more of them to take over human bodies. He systematically replaced people and eventually put our one of our most prolific leaders as the head of the organization."

"Enrick," Angela replied. "We have met."

"He is a ruthless person," Hurt replied. "Chosen as the head of this mission for his ability to focus on the needs of our people over all else. With him in the lead there can be no reasoning and no compromises."

"So, what does this Nemesis mean?" Angela asked. "What does it have to do with the plan?"

"Nemesis is why we wanted to come in this direction," Hurst explained. The terrain changed to show a mighty river ragging though rocky canyons.

"There is a star on the outmost regions of your perceptible universe. It was likely made the same time as your sun and they share a certain … resonance. In this scenario, there is a massive reservoir which is nemesis and the river is the fast-flowing current that leads to the lake at your end, that is your solar system. Though both stars are separate they are connected in a way that your earth scientists no not fully imagine."

"And in ways that have been suppressed, I would guess," Angela added.

"That is one of the primary things NASA needs to hide," Hurst explained. "Were your people able to detect these signals in their fullest they would be privy to all manner of signals, including the transfer of our people themselves. A thing that takes much time and … bandwidth to do."

"What is the craft hidden in space?" Angela asked. "I have seen it appearing and disappearing."

"That is an excellent question," Hurst replied, the scene shifting back to the car on the side of the road. "It is the craft that the first of us ... the one we now call the last scout ... crashed on the moon. Many subsequent lunar missions were made in secret, long after the publicized ones were over to repair and retrieve it. It was retrofitted and used to greater help us bring our people to this place. It is the only part of our advanced technology that is currently here."

"What does it do?" Angela asked, looking at the car as it transformed into a sort of old style supercomputer.

"We have never tried to take over a world this far away before," Hurst replied. "But with the amount of people and their breeding capabilities it is ideal and a destination we will not soon need to leave. We have committed great time and resources, abandoning other searches in favor of this. Due to the distance, we were unable to send many, risking losing subjects with the long trip. The small craft was converted as a sort of way station, a safe place for the consciousness's to stop and wait for a suitable host to be found. That way if there is an issue or an interruption the transfers can be done when it is ready. Up to three of us can be stored there at a time. We have a limit to how long we can stay in the incorporeal form but with NASA's power, what it is, the time is useable."

"Can you tell me what is going to happen that makes things about to accelerate?" Angela inquired. "Enrick said that the time was soon."

"We are currently just out of range for direct transfers," Hurst explained. "Within the year, we will be able to use nemesis and your sun to make a direct link with a receiver on earth. With that we can transfer people non-stop and create a steady stream, then an invasion force. With our people in key paces we will be able to replace people at an astounding rate. By the time that the public at large catches wind of it, there will be no way to stop it."

"Where is this facility?" Angela asked. "The earth-based receiver?"

"That I cannot tell you," Hurst admitted. "It is a secret so protected the others would know if I revealed it. However, I have given you enough information to hopefully inform your next moves."

"Which one were you?" Angela asked. "When did you come to earth?"

"Me?" Hurst said, walking around the computer system as it turned back into the car. "I came here in the long-range vessel, I am the last scout."

"Why would you want to betray your people?" Angela asked. "You risked your very existence to find this place."

"Because I never thought that I would find it," Hurst said with a laugh. "What I told you earlier about having enough life was the truth. Myself and my partner have lived countless lives and we were both so sick of living that we wished for death. However, in a race that prides survival over all else, it is the greatest sin to manually end your life. So, when volunteers were needed for the probes I volunteered. I said my goodbye to my counterpart and chose the riskiest of trajectories. I waited in the vastness of space, lost and surrounded only by silence and my thoughts. I knew that I grew ever closer and closer to oblivion and I wanted it. I soon would be at peace and I would not have to let my people down to get it. When I crashed on your moon I could feel that my time was over. Though my desire was taken from me, as your people found me, I was again bound by my duty to my people."

"You have been with is for so long," Angela admitted. "You do not look old enough."

Hurst nodded. "I am afraid to admit that this is not my first host body but I am hoping it to be my last. I want to die when it dies. I just need your help to do it."

"What changed?" Angela asked. "You said that you had to follow your duty. What made you decide to help me? Why do you want the plan to fail?"

Hurst walked around, looking at the sky. "This planet. We were always told that any planet is a temporary home ... the only worth is what resources and species we can take and use. We were told to never enjoy anything for long and to expect change at every corner. Even taking a partner, a thing forbidden and mostly forgotten by my people. We cannot breed but some of us sought for something above normal conquest. My first years here I felt sadness and emptiness, getting lost in my work and doing what I was supposed to do. However, by the time the plan began to come into fruition I realized something … I liked this place. I enjoyed the cultures, the peoples, the art. When my partner came here I showed her what I had found and she came to love it like I did. We decided that we both wanted to die here, as humans. That is why we are helping you and doing what we can."

"Well I appreciate it," Angela replied. "I just hope I can make sense … of this."

"You have done things that no one else has," Hurst admitted. "You have not only infiltrated the organization deeply you have learned so much in the short time you have had to work with. I would not have told you what I did had I not expected that you could do it. However, we have been at this too long. I must return before I am noticed. You will awaken with Yuri. He has been watching over you."

"Thank you," Angela said with a smile. "For everything."

"It is what I must do," Hurst said with a nod. "I hope that someday after this I can tell you everything."

"Until then," Angela replied with a nod as the world around her faded away and she began the flow toward consciousness yet again.

***

Angela debriefed the others and then spent the next few days in disbelief. She had a lot of information to take in and then decided that it was likely more than anyone could take in such an easy sitting. Octan and Hina took to it quite easily, but they always had a certain detachment from the real world and it helped. Gormanski was quite shocked, having lived so long in a state of trying to prove there was more out there to be presented with all the answers was more than he could take. He, like Angela, was quiet, trying to figure it all out. Yuri made a few jokes, seeming to push the grander implications on what he had heard deep down and not deal with it any more than he could.

Angela was at a crossroads with her plan. She had as much information as she was likely to find and did not know what to do next. She set the others on the search for this ground based installation as she mostly kept to herself to think of a plan. Hurst insisted that the way to stop everything was with what he told her, but she had no idea what that meant. What was said in the vision was like a dream and none of it felt as real as it should. She did not know if she could trust her mind and memories of it. She did not want to risk everything on something she might have simply misinterpreted.

As the rest of the team searched, she did her own investigating. She had a lot of access to NASA's archives and was just going through it to see if anything caught her eye. She noticed that there was another astronaut, a little younger than her, that had been marked for further observation. The woman's name was Alice Able. She had just come back from a mission, and was just out of debriefing and recovery. She thought of herself, when she had first come back and how she tried to reconcile what she had seen. She decided that she wanted to meet this woman, wondering if she had seen something and she needed someone to validate her. Angela would have loved having someone sympathetic back then and decided to arrange a meeting. She sent an email out, claiming she would love to meet up with her and discuss things for a possible book.

Two days later she was meeting with Alice in a coffee shop near the headquarters. She looked up as she entered and she reminded her a lot of herself. She was young, athletic and with long hair. The pair could be confused as sisters, they were so alike.

"Angela?" Alice said with a smile. "It is so cool to meet you!"

"Pleased to meet you too," Angela said as she gestured for the girl to sit down. "How are you readjusting to earth's gravity?"

"Never realized how strong it was until I was out of it," Alice replied. "It's like getting out of bed after a long day of running … everything hurts."

"Oh, I know that," Angela said with a grin as Alice got comfortable. "So, what kind of research did you get up to up there?"

"Mostly micro-botany," Alice replied. "It is my field. There are a lot of plants that are really limited by earth's gravity and we wanted to see if they would flourish in zero g."

"Any interesting findings?" Angela asked, playing with a small notepad and a pen. She played with different tactics in her head on how to ask what she wanted to ask but did not know how to broach it.

"Not as of yet I'm afraid," Alice replied. "The experiment is taking place over three missions. I won't be there to see the results, so I can only wait for the results to be posted. I am hoping to be up on one of the missions but it's not guaranteed if it will be one where the experiment ends yet."

"Ah that's a shame," Angela replied. "Nothing seems as vivid or vibrant once you are back down here."

"No …" Alice replied as she looked up and looked to the sky. It was a thing that Angela did back when she was still confused and curious about what was in space.

"I was once like you," Angela said with a grin. "Being given a ticket to the heavens and then having to adjust to boring old earth. After what I saw my first time, I had no idea what to do about it."

"Saw?" Alice asked, her face betraying surprise. "What do you mean?"

Angela decided to go for the gusto. If she was somehow being monitored by NASA she could write it off as a logic trap.

"The anomaly … many of us have seen it. There one moment … gone the next."

"I thought we weren't supposed to talk about stuff like that," Alice asked. "That is was like our eyes playing tricks on us or something."

"Some would tell you that," Angela replied. "What does your mind tell you about what you saw?"

"I don't know," Alice replied, her eyes darting around. "I am not sure what I even saw."

"You can tell me about it," Angela replied. "I once was in your exact position. I saw something that I could not reconcile and did not know who I should talk to or if I should talk at all. What I can tell you is that you can trust me."

"I do trust you," Alice replied with a reassuring smile. "You are one of my idols … I followed your research from your missions very closely. Is it really ok to talk about?"

"To me it is," Angela assured. "Tell me anything you are comfortable with … I assure you there are people out there that are like minded."

"It was like a translucent ship," Alice admitted. "I saw it very briefly, but no one else did. I thought I was crazy but I can't get the vision of it out of my head. I did some google searches but you would not believe the bullshit on there."

"I can imagine," Angela responded.

"I have an eidetic memory," Alice continued. "I have drawn it and am pretty sure that I can identify it if I had access to some records. Have you seen it?"

"Yes," Angela replied. "A few times. I also have gotten a recording of its signal."

"A strange radio signal?" Alice asked.

Angela nodded. "Have you heard it?"

"Part of it," Alice replied. "There was this strange signal, but we got a call from mission control ordering us to radio silence just after we reported it. We didn't know what it was, but I am pretty sure we were not meant to hear it. I tried talking to our radio engineer about it but she pretended he had heard nothing and the radio silence was a scheduled drill."

"That happens a lot," Angela admitted. "There are actually two lines of thought on such things. There are those would decide who can and cannot have access to knowledge and some that believe that it is for the greater good that this kind of thing be open and shared. Where would you fall on that moral dilemma?"

"I guess I would prefer that all information be shared," Alice admitted. "That kind of covering up doesn't feel right to me. It feels like they are trying to keep a secret and it can't be anything good."

"I agree," Angela said with a smile. "I have a group of individuals that are of the same boat and we would love to get together and share information with you."

"That would be great," Alice answered with a smile. "I would love to find out more and really enjoy the chance to work with you."

"We are actually based in the city," Angela replied. "We have …"

Angela was interrupted as Alice's phone went off.

Alice took out her phone and mouthed an apology to Angela. "Hello … oh yes … oh, I will take care of it at once…"

"Is everything alright?" Angela asked as Alice hung up her phone.

"Oh yes," Alice said with a smile. "I am helping my gran with her health issues. That was her pharmacist and he needed to readjust her pills. I have to go over and pick them up a block from here."

"We can talk another time," Angela said with a smile. "I will contact you about the other stuff … but in the meantime, keep it on the down low."

"I will," Alice replied with a nod as she got up and headed out.

Angela felt pretty good about the whole thing. She felt like she had found a kindred spirit and it reminded her why they were doing what they were doing. There were too many people swept under the rug and silenced and it was good that she had gotten to another one first. She left the coffee shop, already making plans to invite Alice to the headquarters and introduce her to the others. As she walked she head some shouting from down the street. Angela looked at the direction and could not see much. Moments later some emergency vehicles went by and she started to feel a strange sick feeling in her stomach. She turned and began to head toward the direction of the disturbance.

As Angela got closer she saw the traffic stopped and emergency personal clearing an area. She looked ahead and saw the sign for the pharmacy beyond the chaos. Angela knew that something was wrong and she moved closer as a grizzly scene unfolded to her. It seemed like a garbage truck had lost control and gone off the road and into the parking lot of the pharmacy. It was now smashed into the building and being taped off by local authorities.

"What happened," Angela asked to a witness who seemed to have been there for it. It was a young man with a dog.

"I ain't never seen anything like it," the man replied. "The garbage man had just gotten out to help the guys in the back and the truck took off like it had a mind of its own. I didn't know garbage trucks could move that fast."

"Was anyone hurt?" Angela asked, desperate to be told that there were no casualties."

"Took out a lot of cars like they were nothing," the man explained. "Everyone got out of the way … well except for that girl … poor thing … she kind of looked like you."

Angela's heart sank and she became mired in an oppressive sense of dread. She simply ran from the man, closer to the truck. She had to be sure. As she got closer, the police stopped her at the perimeter. She saw blood coming out from the front of the truck. She searched for some manner of evidence that it was not Alice, but that is when she saw it. Alice's phone, tossed several feet away by the impact and laying on the ground. Angela did not think, instead moving over to where the phone was and hoping no one else had noticed it … or her yet. She reached out, took the phone and immediately began to walk away. Had it been her that had gotten the girl killed? How had NASA planned such a freak occurrence? It was definitely not a coincidence … she did not believe in coincidences anymore. Feelings of fear and paranoia flooded into her head as she wondered how much had been compromised. Were her fiends in danger? Flashes of her group meeting similar gruesome ends flashed into her head and she had to force them out. Angela got a block away and into an alley as her mind spun too fast to deal with. She put her hands to the wall and threw up on the concrete.

Angela had allowed herself to grow a protective bubble of sorts around herself so she did not have to see the danger and the reality of the things around her. However, she was given a grim reminder of just how ruthless NASA was and she needed to double back and recheck her ground. She would go back to headquarters and check on things … there was much work to be done … more so because of all this. However, she decided that for that moment she would take a little while … allow herself to calm down before logically facing what had just happened. All she knew is that she allowed herself to think that things were different … this would not be a mistake she would ever make again … things could never be the same … not after this.

***

Angela spent the next few days on a kind of autopilot. She could not help but feel responsible for what happened and nothing seemed to make sense. When she returned to headquarters, she was paranoid and worried that some manner of accident would befall everyone else. However, no such thing happened. It seemed by all reckoning that NASA was completely unaware that Angela was involved and if so, it was likely that she was just too late to evaluate her before the hit was supposedly ordered. Angela knew that there was so much to do, so much to plan and so much still left to figure out. She knew that the group was due for a mass meeting, a briefing for what was to be done. She laid in bed as the sun rose in the sky. She always prided herself in being a perfectionist that could get the job done no matter what. That was before ... back when she thought she was made of Teflon and nothing could affect her. All she could see now was her own fallibility and how fragile her position was.

There was a knock at the door, she knew it had to be someone come to see if they could get her to the briefing. She expected Octan, or Yuri when she answered. "Come in."

Gormanski stepped in, an awkward look on his face. "Sorry to bother, just wanted to check in on you."

"I suppose this is where I assure you I am fine," Angela replied, not getting up.

"We both know that isn't true and it is not what I really came here to say," Gormanski explained. "I came to tell you a story."

"Is it some sort of analogy or clever anecdote meant to inspire me?" Angela asked. "I think I am far beyond any realm that inspiration can reach to be honest."

"No, nothing like that," Gormanski replied. "Mostly I just wanted to tell you about something that happened to me ... if that is alright?"

"Go for it," Angela replied. "I am fairly indifferent at the moment."

"Well, I would tell you about my wife," Gormanski began. "A topic I do not speak much about."

"I didn't know that you were married?" Angela asked, admitting to herself that she actually knew very little about Gormanski.

"Well, we weren't technically married," Gormanski replied. "What you do know is that I was part of a research team trying to prove the relation of gravitational co-ordinates and their significance. Anna was another researcher and perhaps one of the few people that I worked with that I felt any real affinity towards. We started out as simple colleagues but as the study grew so did our relationship. It was not like a normal courtship, there were no dates or romance, just experiments and equations. However, as all this went on we grew closer and closer. We decided that we wanted to be together forever and planned to get married after our research was done."

"That actually sounds really cute," Angela commented, admittedly becoming captivated by the story.

"As with many projects it dragged on and on and we decided we could not wait," Gormanski said, a look of amused melancholy on his face. "We had an impromptu ceremony in the lab and even had the papers ready to sign to make it official. However, that was when the unthinkable happened."

"NASA shut you down," Angela interjected.

"Exactly," Gormanski continued. "It all happened so fast, one day we were respected scientists and physicists on the verge of a cutting-edge discovery and the next moment we were frauds. NASA decided, though, we were not worth silencing manually it was our reputations they wanted to destroy. We all lost our grants, our accreditations and some of us were hit with multi-million-dollar infringement lawsuits for patents that the ink hadn't even dried on yet."

"That is their modus operandi," Angela admitted. "Scare you, destroy you or kill you."

"I knew that I could not be shut up," Gormanski admitted. "No matter what they threw at me, I knew I could persevere, however my colleagues started dropping … giving up or giving in … and Anna."

"What did they do?" Angela asked. "What did NASA do to Anna?"

"Nothing directly," Gormanski replied. "Other than their deceitful tactics. But something in Anna changed. It was like all the life was drawn out of her and she grew more and more distant. We never got around to signing the papers, forgotten under the chaos of what was going on. I just figured that we would eventually come out the other side and things would go back to normal … until one morning … Anna stepped out in front of a subway train."

"Oh, my god," Angela said as she sat up. "I'm so sorry Gormanski … I didn't know."

"I am not sad," Gormanski added. "I grieved. I took my time. There is no more sadness in me, only anger and determination. This is why I am still at it. This is why I will never willingly give up the fight against them."

Angela nodded, realizing that by killing and destroying people, this was NASA's ultimate plan. It was not just for those that were affected, it was for all those around that saw it and became afraid by proxy. Angela focused on something past her fear and sadness, finding the white-hot rage inside, the thing that would drive her on.

"You are right," Angela nodded. "This is not the time to be sad. This is the time to get even."

"Normally I would not condone such negativity but it is really strong when you let it be," Gormanski explained. "The people out there need you."

"I know," Angela said as she stood. "Let's get back to work."

The group perked up as Angela walked onto the living room. They all had looks that were a mix of relief and concern. They waited until she sat down and got her laptop out. She looked around.

"Ok what do we have?"

"Well we have some reports of NASA shuffling around some serious money," Octan replied. "Such a big amount that there are currently holds on all spending on the corporate account."

"I am trying to figure out where it is going and managed to put a trace on one of the transaction," Hina replied. "We don't know what it is just yet, but once the accounts balance themselves, we will know more about how it ended up."

"Good," Angela replied. "This earth based array will take some serious resources and they likely will be paying for it. There will eventually be a pattern big enough for us to pinpoint it."

"I got a lot of rumors about secret tech being commissioned," Gormanski added as he sat down. "So far most of it is conjecture but some of it might fit into Hina's pattern."

"I would like to add something I have discovered," Yuri broke in. "I know I have not been able to contribute much but I discovered something interesting."

"We're all ears," Angela said with a smile. "What is it?"

"I think I have a way to tell who is an alien or not." Yuri replied. "It is still a theory."

"That's amazing!" Gormanski said with a surprised look. "How did you do it?"

"It was an accident mostly," Yuri explained. "With all this going on I started carrying ... other ways to communicate. They have ways of tracking modern smartphones ... as Hina will tell you. I have since been using an older analogue phone. It is simplistic but a lot more difficult to track."

"I did not know those still worked on modern networks," Hina admitted.

"Surprisingly they do," Yuri explained. "They upgraded most of the older networks and they still function ... well at a limited capacity. It is good enough to use as an emergency phone that is difficult to pinpoint. Angela and I both had our smartphones off for the meeting but my analogue one was left on. It started going haywire in my picket the second we were within ten feet of Hurst."

"Really?" Angela replied. "That's amazing? Could it be from some other kind of jamming."

"Unlikely," Yuri continued. "It was fairly light at first, but as you went into that hypnotic state it nearly fried the phone ... I had to turn it off."

"It must be reacting to whatever extrasensory fields are linking them together," Gormanski theorized. "Happening to use similar frequencies."

"I isolated the frequencies the phone was using and cloned it to this device," Yuri said as he showed a small jury-rigged device. "This will just vibrate when it reacts to the signal … well next time we see it."

"How is it that the aliens don't know about this?" Octan asked. "They are literally in position of the most advanced technology on the planet."

"It's too low tech," Hina theorized. "It is literally too far below them to be noticed."

"Could this be used to hurt them?" Angela replied as she looked at the small device. "Disrupt them in human brains."

"I'm not sure," Yuri replied. "Hurst seemed completely unaware of my device. He was likely sending out a monumentally stronger signal. Perhaps if we could match the intensity, it might affect them but we'd have no way of knowing."

"It is definitely worth looking into," Angela said. "As soon as you can see about putting the device together."

Yuri nodded. "Now keep in mind that this is just a theory. I am still not entirely sure it was an alien mind signal that triggered the device … there is no way to really check."

"Uh, maybe there is," Hina replied. "I just got a message for you Angela though the secret NASA channel. It is Enrick … he would like to speak to you."

"Do you think this is a trap?" Octan asked. "That is awfully sudden."

Angela smiled to Octan. "I am done being paranoid … I'm back into fight them with all I have mode. Tell him I'm coming in … it is time to test the device."

Angela drove to NASA headquarters, gone was her uncertainty, gone was her fear. She was back on track and like an unstoppable freight train. She wanted to know if the device would work. She played with idea of what if she was asked about it but the thing likely was too low tech to make much notice.

Sure enough the device did not even cause anyone to see it or care as she went through security. She had it on in her pocket as she was shown into Enrick's office. Angela paused, seeing the man on the other end of the board room. The device stayed silent … she was not close enough.

"You wanted to speak with me sir?" Angela asked, hoping Enrick would come closer.

"Indeed," Enrick replied. "I must admit that I was skeptical when you came to me, but in such a short time you have proven to be quite invaluable. It seems that no matter what is going on you are consistently on top of it."

"NASA has taught me to watch all the angles," Angel replied with a smile. "It has been a really fulfilling challenge."

"I can tell," Enrick said, turning and walking toward Angela, the device, as anticipated began to pulse in her pocket. "Though I know you … you are an explorer. You can feel the call to go back up."

"I would be lying if I said I did not," Angela replied, meaning that part very much. "Is there a mission?"

"There is," Enrick replied. "We are … concerned that some very important astronauts might have seen too much. I want you to go up … talk with them … earn their trust and find out what they know."

"Can we not just simply silence them?" Angela asked.

"These ones are very important to various operations," Enrick explained. "We would prefer not to have to so we need to know."

"You can count on me," Angela insisted. "May I request to take Yuri up with me. He has proven invaluable to my investigations and I have flown with him before."

"As you wish," Enrick replied as if the million-dollar cost mission was something that required so little thought. "You have proven you can get results. As long as you keep this up you will be able to ask for any-thing … within reason."

"Thank you," Angela replied with a nod. "I will endeavor to

maintain my level of efficiency on this mission and beyond."

***

The next few days were a blur of work and activity. Angela arranged for her friends to come to mission control in Kirgizstan at a NASA facility prepping for the next launch. Gormanski and Octan were there under assumed names, a task that Hina was growing increasingly skilled at. Yuri and herself were being prepped for the launch which Angela realized was only in four days. Usually astronauts were given a much longer timetable to prepare, even veterans like Angela and Yuri. It seems NASA was quite concerned about this team and needed to know as soon as possible if they were still on the same page. This of course worked out well for Angela and her team. They were potential allies and they were front row to something NASA was really concerned about.

Each of the members of the little group had one of the devices and in their first day detected no fewer than six aliens in human disguise. Gormanski, Hana, and Octan were given the title of mission preparation analysts and tasked with readying anything Angela and Yuri might need for the mission. The group was given a private boardroom to do their work and they got together for a briefing on what Angela's next part of the plan is.

"Are we sure we can talk privately here?" Gormanski asked. "We are literally in a NASA facility."

"This is the most privacy you have ever had in your life," Hina replied. "This is literally a place that fights against eavesdropping and recording. This room was made to be a private room and if anyone was recording … they would report it to a security specialist … which I am."

"Oh," Gormanski commented. "That is convenient."

"We should get down to business," Octan commented. "I thought we would have more time."

"We usually do," Angela commented. "Though this is literally the definition of a special case."

"So, what is the plan?" Octan asked. "What is our angle."

"We are going to destroy Hurst's ship," Angela said. The rest of the group went quiet in disbelief, thinking that she may be joking.

"How?" Gormanski asked in disbelief. "This is a literally invisible spaceship that is … in space!"

"The ship is within a hundred meters of the ISS," Yuri added, clearly having been briefed to this plan already. "It is well within the range of orbital movement packs and tethers. The only real challenge is what we blow it up with."

"Yeah like how you get a bomb into a solus capsule?" Gormanski said in a tone meant to emphasize the absurdity of the statement. "They don't even let you bring shoes on some flights and you think you can get a bomb into a suborbital rocket?"

"That is where you come in," Angela said as she started dropping huge binders onto the table, seven in all. "These are complete inventories of every useable component on the ISS combined with what we theoretically can bring without suspicion."

"What exactly do you plan for us to do with these?" Gormanski asked.

"It's like Apollo 13," Octan said with a smile. "That is really clever."

"Someone want to let me in on this?" Gormanski replied. "Because if this is a movie reference I am not sure if I get it."

"In the movie, the engineers and scientists had to figure out how to build a lifesaving piece of technology only using the things that were on the mission already," Hina added. "It was a really cool scene."

"Yes, I remember that!" Gormanski commented. "I remember reading … not the scene."

"Oh, it was great," Hanna commented. "Best part of the movie."

"So, we need to figure out how to take components rigged to not explode or cause fire and find a way to make them catch fire and explode … in space," Octan asked.

Angela nodded. "You three are the smartest people I know. Yuri and I have to prepare so you have three days to design and test a device down here that we can build in space and set off."

"It is literally ludicrous this task that you are asking of us,"

Gormanski commented. "But we will get it done."

"I have nothing but the utmost faith in all of you," Angela replied with a smile. "Yuri and I have some simulations to do but I will leave this task to you."

"The worst part is that no one will know what we did," Octan commented. "There won't be a movie with Bill Paxton based on this amazing feat of heroics and engineering."

The intensive timeline was a strain both physically and emotionally. Luckily Angela always kept in top shape so she adjusted to the rapid training well. Yuri took a little longer to get going but soon was as ready as ever. The mental aspect of the timeline was a lot harder, the pure amount of information Angela had to absorb was immense. It pushed her eidetic memory to its limits and forced her to use all of her emotional wherewithal to keep her feelings and worries compartmentalized. She did not have time to wonder if her companions were able to pull of the task she charged them with but she could only trust them. The night before the launch she went to see them and hoped for the best.

"Please tell me that you were successful," Angela asked, worried that she would be told the negative.

"Oh, we did it," Octan said with a smile putting a large basketball sized piece of space garbage on the table. "This is it."

Angela picked it up, it felt surprisingly light. "Can we test it?"

"We kind of can't," Gormanski commented. "It literally needs a vacuum to activate and we really can't blow up a vacuum chamber here."

"How does it work?" Yuri asked.

"It has various chemicals that if mixed together, they will explode," Gormanski explained. "However, in a no oxygen environment that explosion is small. This device basically creates a high oxygen environment that will … in theory, create a very brief and very powerful explosion. It uses a gallium bladder to erode an aluminum base and when it fails, it implodes, then sets off the compounds and explodes."

"How powerful will it be?" Yuri asked. "We have no idea of knowing how durable the ship is."

"Well, we have no way of knowing," Hana added. "This is mostly theoretical science with a theoretical bomb."

"How hard will it be to make?" Angela asked. "We might not have much time and space."

"Actually, it is a marvel of engineering," Gormanski replied proudly. "Well, for the time being at least. I don't think it would take more than six hours to build and well within Yuri's technical skillset. This is far less complicated then the detectors he built."

Yuri picked up and looked at the instructions. "Wow ... this IS impressive. Yeah, it won't take long at all."

"I could not be prouder of you guys," Angela replied. "We have done so much with such a small amount of time. This is our first real strike back and I am excited to put it into motion."

"One question though," Hana added. "What happens ... with the organization after this thing goes off?"

Angela nodded. "I was thinking about that. There is a very real chance we could expose ourselves here. Also, there's a chance Yuri and I might be killed. I have left instructions with Octan for an alternate meet up place I have been setting up. After the launch, I want you all to go there and if it all goes sour, you will be safe there. Hana has documents to prove that you were not in on what Yuri and I did so you all should be protected."

"Well, let us hope for best case scenario," Gormanski agreed. "You launch in a few hours ... it is not the time to dwell on the doom and gloom outcomes."

"Agreed," Yuri added. "We need to keep focused and do our job. I admit that might be hard. I was once known for my sense of humor despite the stress, but of late have discovered it has all but disappeared. All that seems to be left in me is fight and survival. We all must stay focused, less we lose more of ourselves."

"One way or another I want you all to know that it has been a pleasure," Angela replied. "Should I see you again soon, then it is moot but I would rather that be said then not."

"We all know how you feel," Octan smiled. "Whatever happens we were one hell of a team."

There were few words that remained to be said, the group dismissed and prepared for what was to happen next. In the morning, Yuri and Angela were in the capsule, suited up and strapped in. With them again was Duff and it reminded Angela of her first mission to space. Both times seemed so different yet so similar. She still had a fear in the back of her mind that she struggled to keep at bay. However, unlike last time, it was not the fear of the unknown or nervousness. This time it was the fear of what they did know was up there and the pressure to do what had to be done about it. All of the planning in the world might mean very little in space. There was so much that could go wrong, so much that could not be accounted for and she had to force herself not to worry about all of it … at least not yet.

As the capsule blasted off, fighting earth's gravity and gaining inertia, Angela felt herself calm down. She loved being an astronaut and all the cloak and dagger work and secret missions had distracted her from it. She could not help but feel better as the ship climbed and the G forces hit her. She felt like she knew she was where she should be and that helped focus her mind into a more clarified state. She looked at her fellow astronauts, remembering how she felt like an outsider the first time she flew with them. However, now she had a chance to get to know Yuri and trusted him as much as any of her companions. She admitted she did not know that much still about the no nonsense Duff. However, she knew he was beyond capable and even if he could not be made to help them, she knew the regular parts of the mission could not be in better hands.

Soon the ship reached outer space and weightlessness began. Angela took over the controls and began to pilot the ship toward the ISS. Out of the corner of her eye she saw a flash, knowing it was a distortion of the hidden ship. She smiled to herself as she thought. "That's right keep hiding … I'm coming for you soon!"

***

After docking it was business as usual. Duff went to work on his checks and busied himself with his duties. Angela knew he was the kind of man that liked to lose himself in his work and he would not be seen much unless necessary. Angela dismissed Yuri to go and start work on the device as she went to talk to the other crew members. It reminded her of her earlier missions, trying to find out if anyone had seen the thing that she had seen and at that time could not explain. According to the briefings there were three members, all from a Canadian research team and all veteran astronauts. The first she found was an older astronaut named Mansbridge who had garnished fame with his tweets and videos while on missions. Angela caught up with him in the exercise area.

"I love your videos," Angela commented as she floated in and grabbed a hold of a support bar nearby.

"Thank you that means a lot to me," Mansbridge replied. "I've followed your career for a while."

"Thank you," Angela said with a smile, thinking if the man knew of her it would be easier to ingratiate herself to him. "What is your team up to. I didn't have a chance to look over your briefings."

"We have a couple big ones going on," Mansbridge replied. "First is a zero G micro-botany experiment. We are mostly just maintaining it and waiting for the resident botanist to come up in a future rotation."

Angela's heart sank. He was obviously referring to Alice and she did not have the heart to tell him what had happened to her. She decided that she needed to push him to continue before she betrayed herself. "What is the other one?"

"That one is very interesting," Mansbridge said with a smile. "We are orienting the satellites to all work together to take on larger signals in times of emergency."

"That is interesting," Angela replied. "That technology sounds familiar."

"It is cutting edge technology from the company that used to be BriarTech." Mansbridge explained. "We never would have gotten access to the algorithms and patents had they not had … their recent trouble."

"Their loss is NASA's gain, right?" Angela asked, admitting to herself that she was surprised to see just how far reaching NASA's schemes seemed to be.

"Works out in the end," Mansbridge said with a smile. "Ultimately I am not really one for corporate red tape and bureaucracy … it is all too Kafkaesque for me. I am more concerned with scientific innovation and the betterment of humankind's understanding of the universe."

"That is why we're are all here right?" Angela asked. "What will we be able to do with this new network?"

"Well we already have it working … mostly," Mansbridge replied. "BriarTech had it pretty much set up before their fall and we are just configuring it and testing it. We think that we can use it to get information from deep space probes and compile them faster. They turn the whole satellite network into a type of neuro supercomputer that pairs with one on the surface."

"Whereabouts on the surface," Angela asked, wondering against hope that she might find the location of NASA's secret receiving facility this way.

"No clue," Mansbridge said with a laugh. "They don't really tell us what it is used for and our ability to log into the network is very limited. They just want us to get it working to peak capacity and hand over the keys if it were."

"Makes sense," Angela said with a laugh, searching her mind and struggling to find a way to bring up the … more pressing matters. She decided to follow the casual nature of the conversation and hope for the best. "Has the anomaly been giving you any trouble?"

"Anomaly?" Mansbridge asked. "Mostly just our eyes playing tricks on …"

"Oh, let's not bother with that," Angela interrupted. "We both know not to talk about it down there but we are up here."

"It is …" Mansbridge began. "It is around."

"It used to be rare to see the thing," Angela commented, her tone indicating that it was fine to refer to it so easily. "Though lately it is more active. I swear the people at NASA control are playing with it more by the day."

"So, we know what it is?" Mansbridge asked. "Because we were pretty quickly shut down whenever we reported anything about it."

"Well you probably realize there is kind of two NASA's, right?" Angela replied.

"The one that works at science and the one that seems to have its own secret agenda?" Mansbridge asked, his voice growing less and less jovial.

"What do you think of that?" Angela asked. "Do you think there should be some accountability?"

"Perhaps," Mansbridge replied, seeming to not be sure the reason Angela was asking. "Though I am just an engineer and astronaut ... I would not begin to know how to do anything about it."

Angela realized she had accomplished her goals, both hers and NASA's. She confirmed that he did indeed see the thing but seemed to be loyal to NASA with a cautiousness approach. She decided that he might make a nice ally, but it would take a lot of prodding and more evidence.

"How does your team feel about it," Angela asked, hoping to use his candor to make her job easier.

"They trust my judgement on the matter," Mansbridge replied. "They don't know what they saw and frankly do not really need to spare it more thought."

She decided that she did not need to know more, she now had to focus on more pressing matters. "Thank you for your time."

"Anytime," Mansbridge replied, all manner of casual enjoyment seeming to be gone from his tone.

Yuri proved to be just as crafty as she had expected. Even in zero G and in a confined space, he had the device built within five hours and exactly to the specifications of the instructions. Angela perked her eyebrows as she inspected it.

"This looks perfect," Angela commented. "Well, at least perfectly like the other one."

"It is a marvellously simple design," Yuri commented. "Seems the design was Octan's originally. That kid has a future ahead of him as an engineer if he were to assert himself."

"He's much smarter than even he knows," Angela said with a proud smile. "I have never seen a challenge he could not defeat."

"Well that is kind of what we do isn't it?" Yuri commented. "And we still got some to come."

"Were there any complications building it?" Angela asked, wanting to cover all her bases.

"The team here is pretty engrossed in their experiments," Yuri replied. "I didn't really even see them. Duff was asking a few questions but I told him this was part of my maintenance duties."

"Would he have any way to know what we are doing?" Angela asked.

"I doubt it," Yuri replied. "I don't think he can tell a bomb from a pipe fitting. It is not in his skillset as far as I know."

"Good," Angela said with a nod. "We have a spacewalk at 0800. Bring it out with us and we do what we came to do then."

Yuri simply nodded, not wanting to put too fine a point on what was to come.

The next day Duff, Yuri, and Angela suited up. Angela did have a few spacewalks under her belt and though it was mostly routine she found it exhilarating every time. There was no way to tell what was up, what was down and if you did not pay close attentions to the things around you it was very easy to lose your bearings. The mission was to replace a series of panels on the outside. Duff took command of the maintenance and it started out normal. Yuri had the device clipped onto his work belt and had a tether to the space station with Duff. Angela had a backpack on that used pressurized gas as a kind of orbital jetpack. After the first few panels were done Yuri gestured to his payload.

"Duff I am going to take a look at the panels on the other side," Angela said over the open com. "I want to make sure we aren't going to find any surprises."

"Affirmative," Duff replied. "Stay in radio contact."

"Confirmed," Angela replied, climbing over to Yuri and quickly unhooking the device from him and attaching it to her suit. She carefully manipulated the controls and the gas jets fired. It was an interesting sensation moving around in zero gravity three-dimensional space but thrilling nonetheless. She came around the ISS to the open area between it and the earth. She had sat down with all the technical specs and tri-angulated the optimal position of the vessel based on what she knew. She overshot the station and headed out toward it. This was the single most reckless thing she had ever done. She was literally about to come into contact with an invisible alien vessel and try to blow it up. Though she calculated she had ample fuel to return to the station with the back-pack there were literally thousands of unknown variables, many of which could mean death and certain destruction.

To her senses, it seems like she was not moving at all. The massive size of the earth combined with the few points of comparison made her feel like she was floating in place. But as she got closer she saw the telltale flicker of the craft. It became visible, lighting up in front of her. Though she had seen it a few times now it was never this close with this level of clarity. Angela was momentarily taken back in awe at the pure size and splendor of the alien craft. It was bigger than she anticipated, roughly the size of a 747. She snapped out of her awe and shock as she activated the backpack to slow her approach. She would not be able to do what she came to do should she hit it at forty miles an hour. She slowly moved closer, seeing if there was any reaction of the craft to her presence. However, the craft just seemed to do what it was doing, moving slightly to position itself to receive a signal. Angela theorized that it was preparing to receive alien consciousness's and that was why tit momentarily became visible.

She slowly moved closer, her hands touching the craft, causing the iridescent surface to ripple like water. She had no way of gauging the composition of the vessel and therefore could only guess what the explosion would do. She took out a tether from her tool belt and began to lash the device to a small protrusion in front of her. She then pushed down on a lever near the top of the device, setting off the chain reaction that would soon cause the explosion. She did not hesitate, once confirmed it was set she activated the controls of her backpack and began to move away from the vessel. She turned, aiming herself back at the ISS and back to safety.

"Where are you Angela?" Duff said over the com. "I don't have eyes on you."

"Had a minor malfunction with the pack," Angela replied. "It's fine, no need for concern."

Angela remembered the instructions for the device. She remembered that the estimation for time of explosion was about forty-five seconds. However, this was Octan's best guess and there was truly no way to gauge it. She maneuvered herself back as best she could, coming around to where Duff and Yuri were working. She saw the bar that they had clipped onto with the tether and took out her own in anticipation. She needed to be clipped in as the explosion went off, there was no way of knowing what would happen … even with the pack on were she not tethered when the bomb went off.

As she closed in on the surface of the ISS a flash of light hit her peripheral vision, momentarily causing glare to flood her visor. She felt her hands hit the space station and she struggled to reach around and find the bar. She knew the bomb had gone off and though there was no way to hear it she knew within seconds the initial shockwave would be felt any second. She found the bar and attached the tether a mere second before she was yanked backwards away from the ship before jerked to a stop violently by the tether. As she came around she managed a look back at the vessel … it was gone and it its place was a literal ball of fire, swirling in space momentarily before succumbing to the vacuum around it. As suddenly as the fire started it was gone, replaced by a dense cloud of debris flying out toward the ISS with frightening speed.

"Something exploded!" Angela shouted into the com. "We need to get back aboard the station as fast as we can!"

"Get to the airlock," Duff shouted as he and Yuri untethered and moved rapidly, hand over hand crawling to the airlock. Angela untethered and used the pack, knowing she had little fuel left but moving with the last of it. As she got close she ejected from the pack, flying to the airlock and beginning the sequence to open the door. Angela moved inside, preparing to engage the airlock cycle as soon as the others arrived. She looked out and waited. The station began to shake violently, pieces of the ship striking it and scratching against the hall. Angela was tossed from the door, she struggled to grab hold of something but there was nothing. She felt a powerful arm grab her. It was Duff. He had one hand on the airlock door and one on her. The space around them swirled as the station seemed to spin at place. Duff strained and pushed Angela back through the door where she was able to grab onto a bar and steady herself. Duff came around just as a large piece of debris streaked over, striking him in the chest, puncturing his suit and sending him off spiraling into open space.

"Duff!" Angela cried out but it was too late. Duff would not be able to reply even if he was still alive.

The station shook again, spinning faster and faster, more and more debris from the explosion tearing into the hull of the ISS and causing it to begin to buckle. As the orbital spin intensified, it added an increasing G force to the station. Yuri clung to the outside, unable to move and holding on for dear life.

"The ISS is risking explosive decompression!" The voice of Mansbridge shouted over the open com. "All hands to the emergency re-entry capsule. Team two what is your status?"

"Duff is gone," Angela said, her mind switching to danger mode. "I'm in the airlock but Yuri is still outside. I am going out to get him!"

"No," Yuri replied, his voice remarkable calm. "There is no time."

"I am not leaving you out there," Angela insisted. "I only need a couple of minutes."

"Mansbridge," Yuri responded. "Override the airlock."

"No!" Angela shouted but before she could react the door closed on its own and the depressurization cycle began. She pounded on the door but it was too late. As the cycle completed, Mansbridge came into the compartment.

"We need to go right now!" Mansbridge shouted. "The station has minutes left!"

Angela fought to keep control of her emotions, removing her suit as fast as she could with Mansbridge's help. She then followed him though the station. There were micro-fires and gas leaks. It was as he said, the station was soon to be torn to pieces by an explosive decompression that would rival the explosion that had just happened. Thoughts of her actions flowed through her mind as she struggled against the shifting and spinning station and into the escape vehicle, she forced them back … she would deal with them later … if there was a later. She and Mansbridge were helped into harnesses by the other Canadians and one of them started counting. They needed to be clear of the station before it exploded but also needed to be facing earth at just the right angle. Everything seemed to slow down as if it were a dream. The Canadian astronaut hit the button and the capsule shook. For a few seconds, it was peaceful again, the shaking of the ISS far behind. However, it was short lived as the capsule began to shake violently, experiencing a shockwave as the ISS exploded. The capsule spun around, it was now out of control and only luck and the grace of destiny could ensure that the heat shielded side would be the side that struck the friction heavy atmosphere.

It was the culmination of a chain of events that started the second Angela first saw the craft and now, like the trajectory nothing could stop it now. Back on the ground, if she survived there was still much to do … but everything would be different. As the capsule spun and struck the atmosphere it came to a stop, the lights flickered and for a moment there was only darkness.

CHAPTER SIX
A Moments Hesitation

The capsule streaked through the sky at a speed that many on the surface could only dream of. Luckily the craft had had its heat shielded side to the atmosphere and did not break up from the tremendous friction of re-entry. Most of the emergency capsules functions were automated but that did not stop both Angela and Mansbridge from going over them and watching for complications.

As the capsule got lower in the atmosphere, multiple parachutes deployed and caused the entire craft to lurch as it slowed down. The capsule still shook violently as the forces fought each other and the craft moved toward the ground. Soon ground was visible on the horizons out the window, a vast sea of green, likely field and forest. Angela and the others had no real way to gauge where it was from here and would have to take stock on the ground. Soon the capsule came close to the surface, firing powerful retro thrusters to burn off the last of the speed and coming to rest safely on the ground.

Angela went to work to blow the hatch. She had only been in space a few hours and her body was still used to earth's gravity. However, the Canadian crew had been in orbit for weeks and their bodies were weak and their muscles still acclimatizing for the greater strain. Angela took a scan around and guessed that they were likely somewhere in Europe … it was hard to tell but the vegetation and basic location of the station when it went up seemed to confirm it. She checked the craft for any signs of fire and set off the rescue beacon. She had a thousand questions in her head and eventually would have to sit down and sort through what had happened. Duff was dead, Yuri was dead, the most advanced space station in the history of mankind was destroyed. The question of if it was truly worth it flowed into her head but she shook it off. There would be time to weigh the moral implications of her actions but that would come after the fulfilled her mandate to protect the earth from invasion and enslavement.

As anticipated the Canadians were sluggish and weak. They also seemed to be forcing themselves to compartmentalize what had happened and focus on their training. Protocol said that the first priority was to make sure the capsule was safe. It had the homing beacon and their necessary supplies. Second was to make up a camp. Though it seemed warm enough in the field they landed in, there was no counting for how cold that it would become in the night.

Angela helped set up the camp and prepared to rest. Even with NASA on likely high alert to what had happened, it would take them hours to get there. Mansbridge began to hand out some rations as the group tried to relax and reflect. Angela wondered if she should leave. Would they know what she had done? She wrote off this idea as she did not even know what country she was in and it was probably pointless to think she would get far.

As the sun set, the temperature plummeted. The group huddled in their emergency tent with thermal blankets to wait out the night. A few hours later, lights fell on the outside of the tent and the roar of powered vehicles grew louder. The group cautiously emerged from the tent as several all-terrain vehicles stopped around the front of the campsite. Several figures got out, their identities obscured by the oncoming flood lights.

"Captain Angela McGee?" one of them shouted in an unfamiliar voice.

"That's me," Angela replied, shielding her eyes from the light.

"Confirmed," the voice replied. Movements later gunshots began to go off. Angela instinctively shielded herself but as the shots continued, she realized that she was not hit. She slowly opened her eyes to see Mansbridge and the others were dead on the ground. They had shot everyone but her.

"Come with us!" the voice demanded, stepping into the light to reveal a man in full tactical gear. Angela weighed her options and resized were it not for the man's orders, she would already be dead. She had no choice but to do what he said. She walked over with her hands up and was quickly ushered into a truck. She expected to be cuffed, beaten, tortured but instead a blanket was put over her shoulder and a hot beverage was handed to her in the cup from a thermos.

"Are you alright captain?" the man asked in a voice to casual for a man that just ordered an execution. "If there is anything you need just say so."

"Why did you shoot the others?" Angela asked, trying to keep her voice as calm as she could.

"Orders ma'am," the soldier replied. "I am not at liberty to discuss that. I was just told to find you at the site and take any others out."

"I see," Angela said, holding the warm cup in her hands, struggling not to freak out.

"Everything will be explained once we bring you in," the soldier assured. "You are safe now."

The truck left the site, leaving others to deal with the capsule and the Canadians. Angela knew that what she said when she was brought back to base would be important so she went over things in her head. Part of her was in no state to plan, no place to defend but the analytic patterns made it easier for her to compartmentalize. She began by thinking of what they would know. There were no active broadcasts to the surface so literally nothing that happened within the previous twelve hours on the station was logged. There were recordings on the capsule of what happened but they did not include voice logs and had no idea the full scope of what was going on at the time. All that it would likely report is that an external force struck the station and it caused catastrophic failure. Angela was pretty sure that the only real way they would have to report on what happened was her testimony and she had to make sure it was consistent. She decided that she would see what they knew first and build from that. She needed to be careful or the line between her being a surviving NASA asset and a traitor would become very thin.

Angela was eventually taken to a helicopter and within hours was at a NASA base in Sweden. Angela could not help but laugh as part of her thought that Octan would be very jealous how close she was to Lego headquarters. Though the throw away thought was completely unimportant to her in her current situation, she took solace in this small thought of her friend. She would need to conquer her fears and uncertainties if she was going to get through this. She could not allow herself to be compromised by trauma and thoughts like her good friend's obsession with building bricks helped.

Angela was checked out by a doctor and given food and a hot

shower. She felt that she was in the best shape that she could be in and was taken to be debriefed. In the conference room waiting for her was Stone. He sat with his ever-present phone in front of him and a laptop off to the side.

"Not many people have survived what you have survived," Stone commented. "You were very lucky."

"Very," Angela replied as she sat down. "Especially more than the others."

"They were compromised," Stone replied. "You must understand that their conspiracy is something that needed to be swiftly dealt with."

Angela nodded, Stone and NASA seemed to already be building their own narrative about what had happened. She could use this to not only protect herself but to advance her position for the oncoming conflict. "I suppose my biggest mistake was taking too slow a tactic to try and weed out their involvement. I had only gotten to one of them before everything went to hell."

"Do not hold too much blame," Stone replied. "They likely had been working on this for some time. There was nothing up there that could have done to stop the damage. We suspected they constructed some manner of explosive device in the weeks leading up to the incident."

"Agreed," Angela said, realizing that her teams speed and ingenuity had absolved them of the guilt. "They all seemed preoccupied and showed signs of knowing about … the craft. They seemed like they suspected that we might try to stop them."

"How did it go down?" Stone asked. "Give me the timeline."

Angela nodded. "Well, after interrogating one of the crew, we did a search. Yuri was unable to find anything within the station and we had reason to believe that they might have done something outside. We had a scheduled task and went out to look for anything … out of the ordinary. I was on a movement pack and decided to take an extended look at the station. As we both know … there is a hidden … asset in space near the station."

"Or at least there was," Stone replied with no sign of covering up his frustration of that fact.

"I had seen the thing before," Angela replied. "As you know, my curiosity led me to my desire to join with the higher Escalon of NASA. Though I, of course, know very little about the classified craft, I knew enough to tell that there was something ... inconsistent attached to it. It was some manner of device and I decided that I should investigate. I understand I did not have clearance for this but you can understand the need for secrecy on this ... so I made a call."

"That makes sense," Stone said with a nod.

"I used the pack to go to the craft," Angela continued. "I did not have the time or tools to truly assess the device but it seemed that it was getting ready to go off. I could not stop it so I tried to warn the others and save the station ... alas I failed."

"That was unfortunate," Stone agreed. "But you had the right instincts. You risked it all and that is the kind of thing we expect from you."

"Duff and Yuri performed beyond expectations," Angela commented. "I want to go on record with that."

"It shall be noted," Stone agreed. "This situation is ... less than ideal. You did your best and we are glad we were able to retrieve you."

"So, what now?" Angela asked. "I assume that asset anything that cannot be replaced?"

"The ... asset as you call it was one of a kind." Stone admitted. "Though it is problematic and unfortunate that it was lost, it is not the end of the world."

Angela could not help but find his choice of words interesting. As the end of the world was in fact the thing she was trying to stop. "It was a rather intense situation. However, I am eager to stay useful to the organization."

"You are like a well-made watch," Stone said with a smile. "You take a licking and keep on ticking. As for the asset ... we were soon getting to the point where we did not need it anyway. It is a setback, but not anything serious."

"So, what is next?" Angela asked, surprised by Stone's apparent candor. "What is my mission?"

"Return to your team and monitor things," Stone replied. "I am sure we will have more things for you to do in the coming weeks but for now, we will trust you to do what you do so well."

"And what is that?" Angela asked.

"Find threats to NASA," Stone replied as he got up. "You have proven to be a great asset and we have done so much with your help. Do not engage for the time being. You find something that is a threat, you call it into me."

"I will," Angela nodded. "I promise."

As Stone left, Angela could not help but break down. All the loss and the pain was intense along with the idea that she might have done more good for Nasa and their sinister agenda than bad. There would be more fights to come and likely things would get worse. But for right now Angela allowed herself a few moments to not be strong. Tomorrow she would compose herself … today she had enough.

***

Angela worried that some hole in her story would be found, but in the days following the meeting with Stone none were brought up. As it turned out there was very little information recovered from the explosion and NASA could not help but use Angela's testimony as the official account of what happened. She had worried that the Canadians would be blamed and shamed but NASA chose to not play that angle at all. They were apparently planning to list it as accidental death more than sabotage as the former meant less questions.

Angela was brought stateside and eventually left to go get some rest and recover emotionally for what had happened. It was easy to think of it as kindness but she knew with NASA's agenda, it just meant that they intended to use her again, and they needed her at her best. She would have to send the signal that things were safe to the others. Likely with what was going on, they scattered to the fallback position and needed to be told it was all clear. However, as Angela walked into HQ everyone was sitting around in the living room and looked up in shock.

"Wait aren't you supposed to be in space?" Octan asked in shock.

"How did it go?" Gormanski added in eager surprise. "Did the device work?"

"Wait you don't know?" Angela asked in shock wondering how they could possibly not know. "Is it not all over the news?"

"No," Hina asked in a confused tone. "There have actually been no reports from your mission. Even in the NASA network they have been very quiet."

"What happened?" Octan asked.

"It's gone," Angela replied as she sat down.

"The alien ship?" Octan asked.

"All of it," Angela replied. "The ship, the ISS, Yuri … all of it."

"Wait, what?" Gormanski asked in shock. "The International Space Station is gone too? What happened to Yuri?"

"The bomb worked too well," Angela admitted. "We had no way of gauging the reaction with the craft. It tore into the station and we had to ditch."

"Oh my god," Octan replied. "We had no way of testing it."

"I know," Angela replied. "I am not blaming anyone … we … did what we did because we had to. It just did not go as planned."

"Yeah," Octan jumped in. "We can't afford to start blaming anyone but NASA. They literally are going to enslave the world and they killed a lot of people."

"The lad is right," Gormanski added. "Yuri would not want us blaming ourselves … he was one of the people who wanted most to fight against NASA and their corruption."

"He died saving me," Angela added. "I could not save him."

"Don't blame yourself," Gormanski added. "You know who to blame and there will be time for tears. Now we got to fight them."

"You're right," Angela agreed, pushing back her thoughts and fears and allowing her determination to take over. "Do we have anything?"

"I think we found the installation," Hina replied. "I cannot be certain yet but all the signs are pointing toward it."

"Where is it?" Angela asked.

"Antarctica," Octan replied. "There was an Australian team that had recently discovered a site that was perfect from ground based telescopes. There is a place referred to as Ridge A that proved to be the best place to get clear images of space."

"Also, there's not really much up there," Gormanski added. "You make an array almost anywhere populated, you will be competing with ground based lights, radio and cell signals and all manner of man-made interference."

"That was the big draw of South America," Angela replied, thinking back to the massive installation she had been before. "It had amazing clarity for receiving and recording the signal."

"Well, statistically, it is a very good site," Octan replied. "But as you know it is not too difficult for people to reach it. Antarctica takes expensive resources and survival training to reach efficiently. Also, based on a percentage, Antarctica has better weather. It is so cold it barely snows and there are rarely clouds. Also, moisture is a serious issue to telescopes and it is legit the driest place of earth. Nothing lives there and few go there. They can do anything there, almost any day and no one will be the wiser."

"Also, the financial records seem to lead to it," Hina replied. "Everything they are making seem to be protected from cold and they are buying up a lot of the airstrips that are close enough to reach it."

"Yeah it all seems to make sense," Angela admitted. "We have hurt them but even Stone mentioned that it is not a big setback in the greater picture. We need to stop more of their larger operations."

"You want to try to blow up their Antarctic base?" Octan asked. "Because that seems like some serious James bond level stuff."

"Let's say that is plan B," Angela replied. "First and foremost, there is the satellite network."

"I am seeing a lot on that actually," Gormanski chimed in. "There have been a lot of anomalies on the world's satellite based networks."

"What kind of anomalies?" Angela asked.

"Well I know you know a fair amount of how the internet works," Octan began. "It is literally the most complicated system aside from a human brain. It is housed on a nearly infinite number of computers and private networks. As much as they are wired and ground based systems to use it, there is also a big reliance on satellite systems. These networks that use the satellites are pivotal and if even one satellite goes down there is a ripple effect throughout the system and people know about it."

"The interconnectivity of the internet is like an ocean," Hina added. "There's an earthquake underwater in one place and there are effects from it felt on the other side of the world."

"Recently, Amazon had one server that went down," Octan added. "Though it was only one location and mostly just cloud storage, they surmised that it effected ten percent of the internet. That means one in five people in the world were affected by it just because they happened to be using at least one site that stored things on that network."

"Ok I understand," Angela added. "We are getting sidetracked."

"Yes of course," Octan replied. "There have been a lot of anomalies and issues with the internet lately. There have been a lot of theories and excuses but they all seem to have one thing in common."

"BriarTech." Angela guessed.

"How did you know?" Gormanski asked. "Hina literally just came to that correlation with piecing together thousands of error reports."

"That's what the Canadian team they sent me up to investigate was working on." Angela explained. "They were shaking down the Briar-Tech network for specific use without being told what it was for. The tests likely corresponded with the issues."

"The timeline makes sense," Hina replied. "If they were putting massive loads on the system then it makes sense that it would cause issues."

"Do you think it might have been damaged at all in the explosion?" Octan asked. "Maybe we got lucky?"

"Doubtful," Angela replied. "The satellites are further apart then the entire width of this continent. Also, if it had compromised the network, they likely would not have written off losing the craft as a minor setback."

"But maybe we can use this," Gormanski replied. "This BriarTech network might be a bigger key to their operations than we thought. I knew a lot of the BriarTech stuff and even heard conspiracies about it with NASA. We all wrote it off as they were snooping around with what NASA was doing and when NASA destroyed the company, we stopped digging. Well it seems they did not want to just shut them up; they wanted to absorb them."

"NASA expenditures and activities had gone haywire when BriarTech announced that system," Hina replied. "It was like it started a fire."

"That actually makes a lot of sense," Angela nodded, the pieces seeming to fit together in her head. "Let me suggest a timeline."

"Go for it," Octan replied. "Many great breakthroughs have come in through thought experiments."

Angela nodded, "Ok, we have signals coming from another planet, amplified by the suns but still not efficiently. We are using the International Space Station to hide a craft that is receiving alien consciousness's, but soon the signals be will stronger and more profound. We have been retrofitting tech on the ISS for this, but it is still in its infancy when, out of the blue, we discover that a civilian company has made a better receiver. We destroy the company and absorb it … gaining control of the network overnight. We abandoned work on our space station network and instead plan to use this one that we literally just had dropped on us. We rush to build a facility to harness it in Antarctica so when the suns align and the signal grows, we can do mass downloads of the others."

"Shit," Gormanski replied. "You just blew my mind."

Angela looked to Gormanski with a raised eyebrow, "Excuse me?"

Gormanski laughed, "You literally took every major conspiracy theory I have been researching and put them all together in a natural narrative that explains and quantifies them all."

"Yeah, I am pretty sure that's it right there," Octan agreed. "That is their plan … well the Earth side of it after all."

"But they got it all figured out?" Hina asked. "Isn't that bad?"

"Actually no," Angela commented with a slowly growing smile. "In fact, this is good news."

"You going to let us in on why?" Gormanski asked. "Because to me this seems like NASA's alien death machine is pretty much done."

"Well, if they used their original plan then it would be," Angela began. "They were building modules for the ISS to be spread to when they were ready for the increased signal. I remember seeing bits on it when Hina and I started working together. I did not know what they were for at the time and I could not presume they weren't for normal use. This had to be their initial plan to receive the signal. However, this was difficult and slow and likely behind deadline. Due to real constraints of keeping it a secret they could only launch so much of it at a time and might miss the signal starting. This system had likely been gone over meretriciously and had no weaknesses that humanity could exploit once they figured out what was happening. However, with the program falling behind schedule they discovered that their work might already be done for them. A billion-dollar company secretly built exactly what they were trying to make. They take it, but since they did not build it they could not test it to ensure there are no weaknesses."

"That is actually brilliant," Gormanski replied. "They are learning how it works as they get ready to use it. There could be a myriad of back doors and weak points that they need to figure out by trial and error."

"And we incidentally forced them to use it as their primary plan," Angela added. "They likely were going to continue to build the ISS based network as a secure backup, but we put a stop to that."

"And BriarTech was a massive company," Octan added. "There surely is some source of information on the system that NASA could not predict and silence."

"They can't plug all the leaks," Gormanski said with a grin. "At least not this quickly."

"We need to look into BriarTech's assets," Angela replied, her tone becoming brighter and more focused. She had a mission, a way forward and this gave her the fuel to relight the fire within her. "Find us something that NASA does not know, something we can exploit."

No more words were said, no more discussion was needed. The group dived into the task on their laptops, feeling the same burning determination as Angela did. They had hope that there was a way to fight NASA and that was encouraging. With all that had happened, they needed good news and this was the best they were likely to get for some time.

***

Though the implosion of BriarTech had been swift there were still a lot of assets that had not yet disappeared. A company the size of Briar-Tech had considerable resources and that does not disappear overnight. NASA used one of its shell companies to take full control of the company and sold off the parts to buy out the rest of the board of directors. NASA undoubtedly took the parts it needed for the network and just let everyone fight over the rest like a pack of hyenas on a carcass. It was easy enough for Hina and Octan to figure out one of these places NASA might need to hold onto and it was there Angela was starting her search. Her plan was to go in, using her NASA clearance and plug in a search device. This was one Washington's main headquarters for BriarTech and housed one of their largest single servers. It was one of the first snatched up and protected by NASA, prized second only to BriarTech's main headquarters in Silicon Valley.

Angela admitted she did not know exactly what to expect as she got to the high rise building downtown. It pretty much seemed like business as usual. There were people working for them, but now instead of Briar-Tech security passes, they said Vetralinx. This was likely the shell used … if it was even a real company at all. The employees seemed like they were just happy their jobs did not evaporate as fast as most of the company did not long ago. Angela had several plans on how to get past security, but the second she waved her NASA ID they enthusiastically let her though. It seemed the security personnel knew who really called the shots and gave her access as if she were an investigator or a federal agent. She thought about what Stone had commanded of her but figured she was safe as the guards did not even record her name.

She went up to the top and followed the markings until she got into the main server room. She had complex instructions on what to do and it was basically plug a specialized drive into a direct USB port in the mainframe and the device would do the rest automatically. Though she was given access to the place like the mayor gives out keys to the city, she knew she could not be sloppy. If someone inspected the device while it was active it might be traced into the groups personal network. As Angela found a port, plugged it in she hid it behind a magazine. She was told that it would take several moments but no precise estimate was given.

"Is there anything I can help you with?" A young man said as she walked over to the server. He seemed to be a junior programmer, not looking much older than Octan.

"Oh. I am just doing a routine server inspection for Vetralinx," Angela replied as if she was trying to be super casual. "Nothing really important."

"Oh, that's fine," the young man replied. "I was just trying to be helpful. There's not much to do around her for me anymore to be honest."

"Oh?" Angela asked, trying to use the potential conversation as an excuse to stand stationary over the occupied port. "Big company like this I'm sure there is a lot to be done."

"Well there … was." the young man replied. "Like I admit I have not been with the company long. Just over a year. But it seemed like when I was hired after my internship ended, we were like reinventing the wheel every day. Like it was hard … so hard, it was like every few days the bosses would plunk down some idea or challenge on us. We would think it was impossible at first but make it work. I felt like Scotty from star trek … I was working miracles and it made me happy."

"What changed?" Angela asked, already knowing all too well the answer."

"Well, the scandal," the young man confirmed. "The company may still be here … well parts of it anyway, but it's like a zombie. Dead inside but still shambling around like it is still a person."

"Yeah it all seemed to happen so quickly," Angela commented. "I work for the people who run this now, but I won't profess to know what went on behind the scenes, but it seemed like it unraveled like a ball of yarn."

"Well, I know there was more too it," the young man replied. "Companies like this don't just come apart because of social justice over some bad emails."

"You are very likely right," Angela replied, realizing she really did not have any reason to pretend to be loyal to this company she was pretending to be a part of. "But how are you so sure?"

"Well, my mother is an investor on wall street," the young kid replied. "The nuts and bolts to how the company changed hands is not just from the emails and the resignations. There was a full-fledged share holder insurrection."

"Doesn't this kind of thing happen all the time with big public companies?" Angela asked.

"They would like people to think so," the young man replied. "People think that there's a group of suits sitting around a table, voting and making power change hands on a daily basis. However in reality, people like that are usually shy to make changes lest they risk their money. Mergers and hostile takeovers people think happened quickly actually were being planned months in advance with clandestine meetings of shareholders that resembled more of a coup de tat."

"That is really interesting," Angela commented, realizing that it might have more to do with the current situation than she thought. "You think the BriarTech dismantling was in the works longer than we thought?"

"I do," the young man replied. "For such a big company to be dismantled thus it would have taken weeks of prepping and maneuvering. The scandal was the lynchpin but how could they possibly known it was coming?"

Angela remembered her mission to take down BriarTech. In retrospect, it seemed odd that she would have been trusted with such an important task. She then realized they likely had several backup plans and she either proved worthy as plan A or became the fall girl.

"That is a very astute observation," Angela said with a smile. "And you might be right."

The young man nodded, "Though I probably should not be telling this to someone who works for the acquisition company … I suppose it can't really get worse for us. This whole house of cards is on an increasingly shaky table."

"Well things might not be as bleak as you think," Angela commented. "You might find that …"

Angela was interrupted as a fire alarm went off. The pair paused and looked around as if trying to figure out of it was a drill or not. However, seconds later an explosion shook the building from below.

"I think we should get out of here," Angela said as she yanked the drive from the wall. She could only hope it had finished its work.

"I agree," the young man said as he gestured Angela to follow him. "This way to the auxiliary emergency stairs."

The pair moved quickly as another explosion shook the building. Whatever was happening was happening very quickly and the building was in real trouble. The young man lead Angela down the stairs as others joined. Smoke began to grow thick and the temperature began to grow in the stairwell. As they got down about half-way the smoke was too thick and it became clear that there was also fire in the stairwells.

"You know the building," Angela asked to the young man. "Is there a way around?"

"I-I don't know," the young man replied, his confidence fading by the second.

"Listen," Angela said in an authoritative tone. "What is your name?"

"Will," the young man replied. "Will Gertz."

"Ok, Will, you need to focus," Angela began. "You know this building … a guy like you has a mind like a steel trap. Think of a way around."

Will nodded slowly, "There's a central column in this part of the building. It is high up but goes down far enough to get us down."

"Alright we are going to get to it and climb down," Angela said as she looked to the others stranded in the stairwell. "We stay together and we work together."

The others agreed and followed Angela and Will out of the staircase and into the building. The smoke was still thick but with the more open floors, it was mostly rising up and was manageable. Angela grabbed jackets and other pieces of clothing that had been discarded and handed them to others. She wrapped it over her mouth as an impromptu filter and helped others do the same as Will lead them through the labyrinthine of offices toward the center of the building.

"There's a food court on this floor," Will replied. "It is open to the central area and we can use it to climb down."

"What if there's nothing to climb?" one of the women asked in fear bordering on hysteria. "What if there's no way out."

"Lady I recently escaped a situation that few people could ever hope to escape," Angela replied. "Getting you all out of this will be easy compared to that."

The woman and the others nodded, given hope if by nothing else but Angela's determination. The group reached the center chamber and indeed it was accessible. It seemed the fire was consuming the other side of the building and the center was still safe … for the time being. Angela looked out and saw that there was a nearly seven story drop towards the bottom.

"What is at the bottom?" Angela asked. "Is there a way out?"

"That level connects to the convention center next door," Will replied. "If we can get down there, we should have no issues finding a way out."

Angela looked out and saw a series of wire statues suspended by wires. They looked to be generic birds but were large enough to be climbed on and close enough together to go from bird to bird."

"Ok, we are going to slide down onto one of those birds," Angela said as she went over to the side and took a fire hose out a fireman's closet nearby. "I will jump to it and attack the hose and one by one you guys slide down like a fireman's pole."

There was some argument over if that was safe but as the building shook again the protests abruptly stopped. Angela looked to Will. "Ok I need to know that you are my right-hand man on this. I have a very important task for you. I would do it myself buy I have to jump down and secure the hose."

"What is it?" Will asked, trying to be brave.

"Once I'm down there, I won't be able to get back so easily," Angela replied as she tossed the hose down as close to the wire bird as she could. I need you to get people onto the hose and encourage them to slide down. You don't have to be brave but you need to make them think you are. People are brave even when they are scared as long as they just keep moving forward. Can you do that for me Will?"

"I think so," Will replied. "I will do my best."

"That is all I can ask of you," Angela said with a smile before climbing up on the edge. She estimated that it was only a seven-foot drop to the first bird sculpture. She had done similar jumps in training but this time at much higher stakes. If she hit it wrong she could injure herself and that would mean no more climbing. Worse yet, she could overshoot it entirely and plunge the seven stories to the ground. Angela forced both of those possibilities out of her head and made her jump. Angela was no stranger to leaps of faith but she had grown accustomed to doing them in zero gravity. However, with the irresistible pull of the earth forces, it became a much deeper maneuver. She sailed through the air, her feet catching first and her hands a split second later. She had made the jump perfectly and landed just right. The statue swung a little but the steel cables held it in place.

The heat was increasing and the building began to groan. One side of the building was completely on fire and it would soon threaten the structural integrity of the rest of the building. Angel reached out, barely getting a hold of the hose and pulling it back to the statue. She tied it off securely and gestured for the others to follow. One by one the survivor group slid down the hose to the first statue. Angela helped them off of the hose and told them to start climbing down. The statues were quite close together and required no more leaps of faith. Will seemed quite proficient in convincing the others to get on the hose and slide down, his bravery seemed to be up to the task and they could focus on what was ahead of them and not behind.

Soon there were no more people at the top, just Will. The others were already climbing down the statues, the first of which getting down to the lower level and managing to get on top of a news kiosk and climb safely to the floor. Angela gestured for Will to follow her and come down the hose. Will nodded, climbing out and grabbing onto the hose. However, before he was even half-way down an explosion from somewhere above shook the building and made the entire frame lurch. Angela was flung back, barely grabbing onto the frame to brace herself. Out of her pocket came the modified drive, nearly falling but catching at the bottom of the statue by it's cords and dangling precariously over the long drop. Will was flung from the hose, falling the rest of the way backwards, striking the statue and flipping off. He barely managed to catch hold of the bottom part on the other side, ending up too far from the statue below to swing down. He groaned in pain. It looked like his leg may have been broken by the impact and he was struggling to stay focused on holding on.

Angela looked quickly to where the drive had fallen. It was hanging on by sheer luck the drop and Will hitting the structure somehow not dislodging it. However, Angela knew that the friction of the plug was the only thing keeping it up and any second it could fall. Angela felt like time slowed and her choice rattled in her mind. She needed what was on the drive, it was the smoking gun that could lead for a way to defeat NASA. However, this young man, barely an adult had his life hanging in the balance. It was literally a case of the direct result of NASAS deeds versus the way to stop them. Angela had told herself that she needed to be heartless, she needed to pick things based on logic and need. Was this one young man's life worth a potential way to save millions … or billions?

Angela began to climb toward Will, the choice being made in an instant. This one man's life was inherently priceless. The moment she started devaluating one human life over another in such a way she loses sight of the real reason why she fought. She would find another way, a plan B. For now she had to save the boy. Angela climbed down to him and pulled him up to her mere seconds before the drive fell off, falling and smashing down on the ground far below. She pulled the boy around so he could hold onto her like a piggyback ride. Most people would not be able to pull off such a daring climb with the weight of two people but Angela was not most people. She had trained her body to be in peak human shape and it seemed for this very moment was why she did it. Before long she was down on top of the kiosk then the ground. She shifted Will on her back before following the others out of the building to the convention center attached to it.

The group joined the main part of the evacuation and was soon taken out of the building and pulled past a perimeter. Angela handed the boy, who was now nearly out from shock, to a nearby paramedic. She smiled at him as they took him away. She turned back to the building and her eyes went wide. Nearly the entire building was encased in flames and she was amazed that they had escaped it at all. There was no doubt in her mind who started this fire and was again reminded the lengths her opponents would go to protect their interests.

***

Back at headquarters the group looked at Angela like they were seeing a ghost. She was covered with soot and ash, but otherwise ok.

"Sometimes I think you are like a superhero," Gormanski commented. "We were literally watching the live feed of that building fire and wondering what we might be saying at your funeral. But bam ... here you are with barely a scratch."

"I got lucky," Angela nodded. "Very much so. What is the casualty count on the fire? How many hurt or wounded?"

"You REALLY don't want to know," Octan admitted. "Seriously you don't."

"He's right," Gormanski replied. "We need to keep focused on fighting back and not get bogged down. Like I said before, there will be a time, but not now."

"I am not sad or scared," Angela replied. "I am really pissed off. I am tired of NASA thinking they can just erase all their problems with no thought as to who gets hurt in the process."

"It is like math to them," Gormanski added. "There's billions of us and we are seemingly infinitely replaceable. What is a few hundred of us here and a few thousand there."

"I know this is kind of a sensitive issue," Hina broke in. "But did you manage to get anything on the drive?"

"I had something," Angela admitted with a sigh. "But I had to choose between someone's life and the drive."

"No one here will hold that choice against you," Gormanski replied. "You are a good person and I would do anything in my power to make sure that never changed."

"Thanks," Angela replied with a smile. "Do we have a plan B?"

"That might prove challenging," Octan replied. "The fire in the building is kind of meant mostly as a distraction."

"Distraction?" Angela replied. "That seems a little severe for a distraction."

"This is NASA we are talking about here," Gormanski added. "They usually go big with this kind of thing."

"They have unprecedented control of the media at the moment," Octan added. "While they are doing, love reports of the fire they are being fed a terror related narrative by NASA. They technically owned the building so it put them in place to say they found whatever they want. However, as this is going on, NASA is aggressively liquidating, destroying and abducting everyone and everything involved with the making of the satellite network. They want to make sure there's no record of how it works, worrying that someone doing exactly what we are trying to do might find a weakness."

"The best and probably scariest part?" Gormanski added. "Is that any news outlet that is noticing their other activities suddenly finds themselves with severe technical problems."

"They control the satellites now," Octan explained. "They have unprecedented control over information. Even more so then before."

"They know there's a weakness," Angela commented. "At the very least know they have no way of protecting themselves yet if there was one. They are really risking people getting wise to this with this move. They are taking larger and larger risks."

"Well it seems to be working," Gormanski added. "BriarTech was defunct before, but not it is like they have been whipped off the face of the earth. Whatever they have left is likely in Antarctica by now or pro-tected much tighter than even we can crack."

"What if we are going about this all wrong?" Hina asked. "What if there is something they missed and they don't even know they missed it?"

"What might they have missed?" Gormanski asked. "These are literally the most thorough people in the world when it comes to stuff like this."

"I understand," Hina replied. "But they are literally dismantling one of the biggest companies in the world. They started by taking it over, sold off anything non-essential and are now stripping it of anything that is a threat. Do you not see the flaw in this plan?"

"The stuff they sold?" Angela asked. "You think there might be a back door?"

"Well, BriarTech was not the only company was affected by NASA's schemes."

"Cozy," Gormanski replied. "They literally assassinated him and his company went into foreclosure as a result of the resulting chaos."

"Well as your friend was hurt there were others that benefited," Hina explained. "BriarGames was a division of the company, relatively small in comparison, but with many titles and decent success. After the scandal RedFinch Entertainment bought them out. Normally such a small gaming company would never be able to buy something so big but it was like BriarTech was having a fire sale for things not related to their big network."

"Did BriarTech have any massive online games?" Angela asked. "Ones that would need the BriarTech network?"

"Oh yes," Hina replied, seeming happy that Angela was on the same page. "They inherited the server access, the coding language and a bunch of BriarTech servers."

"NASA likely did not see this connection," Angela replied. "I even doubt RedFinch knows all of what they have. There might be parts of the secret network that they haven't even discovered yet."

"It's a long shot," Octan added. "They might have formatted it."

"Doubtful," Gormanski replied. "For these guys the BriarTech assets are a gift from god. They would not dare throw anything away."

"Worth a shot," Octan agreed. "This might be the last chance we get to find any intel on the NASA satellite network."

"Where did they take the BriarTech assets?" Angela asked. "Is there a consolidated place where most of it went."

"RedFinch only has one location," Hina replied. "Their headquarters in Philadelphia. I can get you the exact address. We still have another one of those server invaders. You just can do what you did with the last one."

"Good," Angela nodded as she stood up. "I will go now."

"You just went though some pretty harrowing stuff," Gormanski added.

"Time is of the essence," Angela replied. "If we can deduce this, it is only a matter of time before someone at NASA doubles back for loose ends. I need to hurry."

"I am not saying don't go," Gormanski smiled. "I am just saying that you might want to change and maybe take a quick shower. You walk into the RedFinch building like that they might think you were in some sort of accident … well other than the one you were actually in."

"Good point," Angela agreed. "I'm going to clean myself up while everyone gets everything ready."

"One more thing," Gormanski added. "I am going with you."

Angela went to argue but figured it would take monumentally longer than agreeing to let him come. "Alright, we leave in ten."

***

The drive to Philadelphia was fairly uneventful. Angela and Gormanski had little in common and though they were friends where was really little for them to talk about. This suited Angela just fine as talking about things in this environment with little to do might lead to questions about recent events. Angela admitted that she had a very thin wall between herself and the implications of what was going on. She admired Gormanski's apparent ability to make his anger strengthen him. She had had some luck focusing on rage over hopelessness but it was not as strong as his. Angela tried turning on the radio but every station seemed to be pre-empted with news about the massive building fire. She was reminded of 9-11 and realized the terrifying impactions of this new tactic. The previous disaster had captivated the world for some time and no one seemed able to talk about anything else. This would give them as much time as they needed to do practically everything and make sure the gaze of the world was superglued to it. All they had to do is stage another disaster and it would seem to everyone that it was an epidemic. By the time it was over, Nasa would be set up and there would no longer be any stopping them.

The entire situation reminded Angela of a time that she went mountain climbing with her school classmates. They went to a natural park and tried to scale Zeke Mountain. Her group started off well, but as they went and saw how little progress they were making, much of the group became discouraged. When you had come so far and thought you were close to accomplishing something just to discover that there was so much more to go it was debilitating. This applied to the situation now, she felt as if she and her friends had come so very far, been through so much, sacrificed so much. However, when they stepped back it seemed like there was still so far to go. Would they have to go to Antarctica? Would they have to face NASA head on? How did they intend to stop the invasion permanently?

Angela shook this off as she took the exit from the highway. They had made great time, getting to Philadelphia in just over two hours. They followed the directions to RedFinch and soon were in the parking lot. It was late in the evening but there were still lights on. Angela and Gormanski got out and walked to the entrance.

"Any idea how we do this?" Angela asked. "Last time it turned out my NASA credentials got me past security. That won't mean anything to the people here."

"This is the public sector," Gormanski replied. "Money talks here and bravado can get you far. Leave it to me."

Gormanski walked up to the front desk and leaned forward, "I would like to talk to the owner."

"Who are you?" the front desk guard asked. "Do you have an appointment?"

"Appointment?" Gormanski scoffed. "Listen friend, when you get to where I am and make thirty-five million an app, you get to stop making appointments. You call your boss and tell him Jerid Asher is here. If he doesn't immediately tell you to send me up, then I'll walk out and invest somewhere else."

"Invest?" The guard asked, knowing the power of the word in the contest all too well. "I will call him. Please just have a seat."

Angela walked over to the side with Gormanski, "Who the hell is Jerid Asher?"

"He is nobody," Gormanski replied. "But when you were in the shower I told Hina to make a web presence for an eccentric billionaire that invests heavily in upcoming companies that happens to look a lot like me. Whoever runs this place only has to google that name and they will think their golden goose just got delivered to their doorstep."

"Mr. Asher!" a voice said enthusiastically after an elevator door opened. It was a young man in his earthy thirties with short cropped black hair and wide rimmed glasses. "I am Ian Farrow. I am the CEO and main programmer of RedFinch."

"Pleased to meet you," Gormanski said with a nod, shaking the man's hand. "I am glad to have a chance to meet you."

"What do I owe the honor of this visit?" Farrow asked. "I had no idea you were coming."

"I don't usually like to announce I am coming when I visit companies that … interest me," Gormanski explained.

"Why is that?" Farrow asked. "If you don't mind me asking."

"Well, I have a reputation for rather … impulsive expenditures," Gormanski replied. "If I tell people I am coming they will do their best to make it look like the place is what I want to see. This way I get to find out of your company is the … real deal."

"Oh, we are," Farrow nodded. "I assure you we are poised to become the fasted growing game and tech company of the next quarter. We just got several CT-Fusion servers from BriarTech and with the creative talent we have at our disposal, the sky is truly the limit now."

"That is rather impressive," Gormanski admitted. "Have you had a chance to set them up at all or are they still with the wrapping on?"

"Oh, we got them online already," Farrow assured. "They are plugged in on the fourteenth floor and ready to go."

"Would you mind if my assistant took a look at them?" Gormanski asked. "If your hardware capabilities are as you say it might work perfectly for my big project."

"Big project?" Farrow replied, his eyes lighting up. "What kind of project."

"Cuts right to the chase," Gormanski replied with a grin. "My kind of man. How about we go to your office and discuss it while my assistant takes a look at your hardware."

"Sounds good to me," Farrow replied as he turned to the guard. "Please show Mr. Asher's assistant to the fourteenth floor and give her access to anything she needs."

"Yes sir," the guard replied as he gestured Angela to follow him.

Angela was lead to the fourteenth floor as Gormanski was lead off. She knew that he could likely keep the boss occupied for hours but needed to get to her task as quickly as possible. Angela admitted she did not know exactly what she was looking for, but as soon as she got to the sever floor found the middle section pretty much arranged over several large back machines. They still had the BriarTech logo on them and were on and ready to go.

"I will need to inspect these machines," Angela commented to the guard.

"What is it you will do?" The guard asked.

"What is your level of technical understanding," Angela asked, gauging on how complicated a lie she would have to cook up."

"Uhh …" the guard began. "Mostly whatever is on my Play-Station or smartphone. I am more of a hockey guy."

"That's fine," Angela replied with a smile. "I am just going to hook a diagnostic device to the server so it gauges its full capacity and weighs it against the requirements our upcoming project requires."

"That makes sense," the guard said, probably planning to rely to anything she said in the same manner. "Do what you got to do."

Angela nodded, taking out the hard drive and plugging it into the BriarTech server. Immediately the lights on the device lit up, indicating that it was doing it's intended purpose.

The guards radio went off and he put a hand to his earpiece.

"Everything all right?" Angela asked.

"Yeah," the guard replied. "But car alarms are going off in the parking lot. There seems to be something going on and I got to look into it with the other guards. Will you be ok here by yourself?"

"I should be," Angela replied. "Do what you need to do."

The guard nodded and hurried off back toward the elevator. Angela turned back to the device, watching it go. She did not know exactly how it worked but knew that the more lights that came on the more it had worked though it's cycle of cloning what it could. It of course could not clone everything on the server but both Octan and Hina had worked to program it to search for things they needed. Angela had nothing but trust for them but fought an uneasy feeling in her stomach. As before she had learned that there were no real coincidences in this line of work. Though, on the surface, it seemed like advantageous the guard was gone it was just too perfect that it was happening at the very moment she was there.

Angela forced herself to focus, staring at the device as it got three quarters though its process.

"I must say you are the last person I suspected to find here," the voice of Mr. Stone said from behind. Angela turned to find the man had just emerged from the elevator.

"Stone I ..." Angela began. "I am glad to see you."

"Oh, no need for pretense now," Stone replied. "I had expected that you might be too good to be true but this confirms it. There were a lot of convenient things but I wrote them off. An associate of mine seemed to trust you more than he should."

"This was a trap, wasn't it?" Angela asked. "You left this place running knowing full well they had BriarTech server information."

"I suspected there was someone on our side what was not as they seemed," Stone continued. "I admit that I really did not want it to be you. But here you are with your hands in the cookie jar. This is the smoking gun. Only someone who knew our plans, our weaknesses would come here. If you really wanted to protect our interests, you would have called this in … as I told you to."

"So, you are here to kill me?" Angela asked. "If that is it, you should just do it."

"Admittedly I came here to kill whoever came looking for whoever might come looking for this information," Stone explained. "Paid off one of the guards to call me if anyone came here asking about the servers. He called me just after he called his boss. I was waiting nearby and came right over. However, low and behold it was our golden child, our gift that keeps on giving. I would sooner key my Ferrari then destroy such a formidable asset."

"You know I would never join you willingly," Angela replied. "I hate the things you do."

"I never said anything about Will," Stone said as he took a device out of his pocket. It was the same as the device Enrick had used to download an alien into the mind of the man from before. Angela stepped back as Stone smiled. "Oh, you know what this is? You really are much better at this than even we gave you credit for."

Angela went to move toward Stone to get past him but he pulled a gun out of his other pocket. "Not so fast McGee. You're not slipping out of this one."

"I won't let you put an alien in my head," Angela retorted. "I would rather die."

"Then rush me again," Stone replied. "If you so much as move a muscle I will shoot you dead on the spot. You do have a choice and it is live as one of us or die."

Angela froze, she knew how dangerous it would be to have her mind taken over. They would know everything she knew, they would know what the team was doing and could expose them … or worse. The alien could continue to pretend to be her and make them do anything. She knew her only option was death but she could not bring herself to move.

"Just as I thought," Stone replied. "You are strong and resourceful but you just can't so easily choose between life and death. Most people hesitate and that leads to their downfall."

"Not me!" a familiar voice said as a gun shot went off. Stone looked down at himself as a red spot appeared on his chest from a bullet that entered him from behind. He went to talk but found out he couldn't. He dropped his gun and the alien device before slumping down to the floor. Blood began to pool around him as he stopped moving. Behind him was Gormanski, standing with a gun in hand, still aimed at where Stone once stood.

"Gormanski!" Angela said in shock and relief. "You saved me!"

"Why the hell did you think I wanted to come along?" Gormanski said as he put the gun back into his pocket. "Let's get out of here."

Angela nodded, "What about Stone? Can they trace it back to us?"

"You seriously think they would allow an alien in human form to have an autopsy or be looked at by a forensic scientist?"

"Good point," Angela said as she looked to the hard drive. It had finished its cycle and was ready to go. She carefully put the drive away before crouching downs, taking Stone's gun, cell, and the alien device. "There's no going back now. We got to take the fight to them."

"About damned time." Gormanski agreed as he hit the button for the elevator.

CHAPTER SEVEN
Decompression of Thought

Angela had no way of knowing if NASA knew what she did and what happened but she did not much want to wait to find out. Stone was dead, the alien within him no long part of NASA's deception machine. This of course would cause ripples to go through the organization as they lost one of their top assets. This was a double-edged sword. Though it took out a vital member of the organization and Angela took herself out from the roster as well … it also meant that they would grow more cautious. NASA was hurting for once and it potentially could make things much harder.

A contingency plan had been put in effect in case they had to go on the run and this was currently the reality of the next phase of the organization. Angela's family cabin was the perfect place to hide. Though Angela technically had ownership of it the place was actually, on book, owned by someone else. It was a tax evasion tactic and something that could not be tracked on paper. The computer side of it was easily altered by Hina and she guaranteed that they were more likely to find Jimmy Hoffa than the cabin. However, Angela suspected that NASA and the networks involved probably knew exactly where jimmy Hoffa was.

The biggest challenge of the cabin was the internet. The remote area was ten years behind in technology and barely out of dialup. Octan and Gormanski installed a clandestine satellite dish and managed to put a network in place to access a rather fast net, while being nearly undetectable. Angela wondered the kind of things that the group could do in the private sector if motivated like this. Once the group was set up and comfortable … as much as they could be they had to set up to plan. With all the work setting up in the cabin, not much had been discussed and there was a nearly insurmountable mountain of tasks ahead of them.

"Do we have an endgame?" Gormanski asked. "Because aside from us being off the radar and worrying for our lives, we probably do not have much time left."

"According to my sources we are maybe weeks away from the signal growing in strength so they can do a mass download," Hina explained. "We need to move fast if we are to stop it."

"We could build another bomb I suppose," Octan replied. "We did a doozy on the one in space. Imagine we could do one that is better on the surface."

"Well, presuming we could just waltz in there James Bond style ..." Gormanski began. "We somehow get past massive NASA security with a bomb big enough to take the building down. We somehow set it up and get out safely and it goes off, destroying the place. Even with all these miracle level things in place ... what is to stop them from building another?"

"Yeah," Hina replied. "Say they lose several of them all they got to do is stop the transfer. The sun is only going to get closer and they build another facility or a pair of them. There's no way we could blow them all up. Their resources dwarf ours, even with all of the money I hid away for us to use."

Angela thought back to her conversation with Hurst. She recalled he had hinted that a way to defeat them was in there ... she just had to see it. She had been wracking her brain on it for weeks but could not make sense of it. She worried that she would run out of time before she figured it out. It seemed like NASA and the aliens had all the time in the world and they had so little with the team. If only they had more time maybe they could ...

"I think I got it!" Angela said suddenly, finishing her thoughts out loud. "What if we didn't stop them before the transfer?"

"I don't understand," Gormanski commented. "Why in the world would we wait for that facility to become operational?"

"Because you guys are right," Angela replied. "We blow it up they might take some losses but they will rebuild. We need them to be successful. We need them to think they succeeded."

"I still don't understand why that is a good thing," Gormanski reinforced. "That means full invasion, right?"

"Not necessarily," Angela replied. "Hurst said that they are committing a lot to this. They need to hurry but they aren't stupid. The first few aliens that come though are likely to be slow as they want to make sure it's safe. However, according to Hina's inventory, the facility should be able to handle a LOT of data."

"Something like a hundred thousand petabytes," Hina added.

"Petabytes?" Gormanski replied. "I am not familiar with that."

"A petabyte is like ten to the fifteen times of a terabyte," Hina explained. "Basically, one Petabyte is a quadrillion bytes."

"NASA apparently has more storage in that facility than any other computer on earth," Octan added. "They likely have been developing the technology for years just for this."

"Then they must be anticipating massive storage," Gormanski replied. "Once the signal is proved safe they some en-masse."

"That is our window," Angela replied, returning to her idea. "They can store a countless amount of alien consciousness's but the remoteness of the facility then proves a problem."

"Even with the massive power and storage of the facility, human beings are not a stackable resource," Octan added.

"Stackable resource?" Hina asked. "I don't actually know that one."

"It's a theoretical time saving construct," Octan added. "You put a lot of something in one space and you cut down the time dealing with it. If you are making soda it makes sense to stack up a crap ton of sugar there. It is based on the idea that the storage of the thing is easier than the act of brining it in as needed."

"Humans aren't as easy to store," Gormanski added. "Especially before they are converted. They will have to bring the humans in in a steady stream to receive the consciousness'. They are literally in the middle of nowhere so it will be their biggest challenge."

"That is why they are buying up all the landing strips that can make the journey," Angela added. "That and I'm sure almost every long-distance vehicle they can get their hands on. They might have the ability to move large amounts of their consciousness's here but they are dependent on the stream of hosts."

"So, there will be a time when they have a massive bulk of their consciousness's here and not enough hosts to utilize," Octan stated. "A moment when all of their eggs are in one basket before they can be put away."

"Exactly!" Angela replied. "Imagine that even fifty percent of their number are in there when we hit it?" Angela theorized. "The loss would be crippling and by the time they got it back online the other half might not be strong enough to make the journey by the time they recovered."

"A crippling blow!" Gormanski added. "I like it!"

"This is our best way to fight them," Angela added. "Once they are in human form they are difficult to detect and no easier to hurt than a human. However, when they are just information they are vulnerable."

"How do you propose we do it then?" Gormanski asked. "Do we blow up … the server or something?"

"It would be big," Hina suggested. "Were talking about an interconnected network of servers the size of a football field or larger."

Octan sighed. "Now what we are looking at the practical logistics of it we might have a problem. Like the space bomb, as powerful as it was only really was big enough to blow up a truck. The fact it was in space surely helped it. However, to build a device big enough to blow up a stadium will either take materials we could never hope to acquire or be so big we could never actually get it there … not to mention past their security."

"Yeah," Angela admitted. "There is no point in taking out a part of it. "Even if we got fifty percent of it there would still be enough aliens left to start a decent invasion. We need to strike it in a way that takes out a hundred percent of the aliens here and potentially hurts the rest in transit."

"Can we do it like that Will Smith movie?" Octan asked. "What about a metaphysical bomb … what about a virus?"

Hina shook her head. "Though I profess to be one of the best virus makers in the world, that's a bit over my head. Even if we could get a virus on the server, past their security and powerful enough to spread, we have no way to tell if it would affect the aliens. They may technically be data but for all we know they could be immune to the virus and we have no way to test or research it. I don't exactly have any way to experiment."

"Wait," Angela paused. "What if we did?"

"You got a digital alien consciousness handy we don't know about?" Hina asked.

"Actually, I do," Angela replied. "Stone was about to have me taken over and we got the device. There is likely an alien in it ready to go."

"Let me see it," Octan asked, taking it from Gormanski and looking it over."

"Also, we have Yuri's research on the alien signals. He seemed to think there might be a way to disrupt them."

"There has to be a weakness in here," Gormanski added. "We just got to find it."

"Where there might be the problem," Octan added. "Because this device may not look like much but it is a technology that I cannot even begin to figure out. This thing is literally alien technology and I can't make heads or tails out of it."

"We can't even hook it up to a diagnostic device," Hina added. "Without knowing how it works, I fear anything I do will destroy it."

"That is a problem," Gormanski replied. "As much as I would love to kill another one of these bastards, that would prevent us from learning anything."

"Well, if we cannot make heads or tails of it we need to go to someone who can," Angela replied. "Is there any indicator on where it was made?"

"There seem to be markers on the machine from a company called Arizona Logistics Limited," Hina replied.

"Yeah, there is a chip on here that says that," Octan replied. "An older one though. They don't make this kind of chip anymore."

"What do we know of this company?" Angela asked. "Where are they based?"

"They seem to not actually exist," Hina replied as she searched on a laptop. "They have no actual presence anyway … or at least anymore."

"I think we might be looking at this wrong," Gormanski added. "We are thinking of a super advanced secret organization like BriarTech. What if it is the opposite?"

"Like it was old?" Angela replied. "They have been at this awhile and the device is quite old."

"Exactly," Gormanski added. "Imagine you are Hurst. It is the sixties and you need to get someone to make a device to simulate something simple from the planet you are from. Back then it is cutting age tech but you get them working. They work and, like a lot of tech back then, they are virtually indestructible. What is the best way to protect it from prying eyes?"

"Let the tech go obsolete!" Octan weighed in. "Let the company you used fall into obscurity and wait for technology to move on so far the original tech seems … alien to modern technicians."

"So, we don't need to find someone advanced enough to read it," Angela added. "We need to find someone who still remembers how this would have worked years ago."

Everyone turned and looked at Gormanski.

"Ok. I realize you all are expecting results from me because I am the oldest one here," Gormanski snapped. "I admit I probably do know a guy but the assumption was unappreciated."

"Sorry," Angela said with a laugh. "But we were right and we very much need to talk to … your guy."

***

When she was working with NASA, it seemed so easy to take a private or commercial jet and get almost anywhere. Though she could still afford to, Angela decided that it was best to stay under the radar and that meant not travelling on commercial flights unless absolutely necessary. For this end, once Gormanski had given information on "his guy" this meant it was time for a road trip.

Gormanski gave all the information on how to find the man and everything they would need. Angela decided to take Octan with her, both because he was most needed to decipher the tech talked about and she had not had much of a chance to work with him lately. The trip took them to New York. The drive was not too long and Angela took the moment to try and enjoy it as much as she could.

Before long the pair was in a parking lot under one of the bridges that lead into Manhattan, waiting for someone who called himself "The Historian."

"I admit that when you watch movies about clandestine operations, they usually skip this part," Octan admitted, his hands in his pockets and looking bored.

"What part?" Angela asked. "Oh, you mean the waiting? Yeah this is like ninety percent of what I do. I ultimately only tell you the fun or dangerous parts in our little meetings."

"Well those are my favorite parts," Octan commented. "Of everything that is good anyway."

"The exciting parts?" Angela asked.

"No, the meetings," Octan replied. "Those, by far, are my favorite parts."

"How so?" Angela asked. "It is just us sitting around debating next moves and pieces of a monumentally big puzzle."

"It is wonderful," Octan commented. "You ever wonder why I never talk about my parents? The fact that I pretty much moved into HQ and started working for you twenty-four seven."

"I kind of wondered," Angela commented. "I admit though the thoughts of that fell a little under the wayside with … everything that is going on."

"Well look at it this way," Octan offered. "I left and moved into the HQ months ago. My parents have not noticed yet."

"You have to be joking," Angela replied. "I am sure they noticed."

"My mother is a stock broker that spends more time in Japan then stateside," Octan admitted. "My father is addicted to every drug that can be prescribed legally. I proved from a young age that I can take care of myself and they kind of embraced it."

"That's good, right?" Angela asked. "A lot of people your age would love the freedom."

"Oh, I do," Octan commented. "I just wish it didn't happen the way it did. I didn't start out so independent. My parents were a functional parental unit for like six years, then it declined year by year. By the time I was twelve, my father could not be relied to feed me and my mother could not be coaxed to caring. I had only my computer … I taught myself to code and how to make money off the internet."

"I'm sorry," Angela replied. "I didn't know."

"I don't blame you at all," Octan replied. "I kind of was not in a great place. I told you that I learned how to make a living on the net … I am not speaking about designing websites or software. I am talking about identity theft. To be honest … when we first met, I was trying to get information from you. But you went and just offered me money … money to do something much more interesting and proved that I can make good by my skills."

Angela laughed. "I suppose we both lucked out then. I got one of the best accomplices I could have asked for."

"Well, you gave me something that no one else ever had," Octan replied. "And I am not talking about the money … you gave me a sense of worth. You relied on me and with what I did for you, we made change. That is invaluable more than anything else."

"I would not be where I am without you," Angela said with a smile. "You may be neglected by your family but we never will … well as long as we don't get assimilated into an ancient spacefaring culture of digital consciousness aliens."

Octan laughed. "True enough. You are like a sister to me."

"I don't have a brother," Angela replied. "But you are what I imagine one would be like."

"This is like an after school special," an unfamiliar voice chimed in. "I don't know whether to get a boner for how sentimental this is or how awkward it is that I didn't speak up earlier."

Octan and Angela looked over to see a tall thin man with white hair and thick glasses. He was dressed in some dress shirt and slacks with what looked like a house coat overtop.

"The Historian I presume?" Angela asked, standing up straight and walking over. She offered her hand to shake. "You can call me Solitaire, this is Octan."

"Nice to meet you," The Historian said as he looked down at Angela's hand. "I don't touch other people for any reason."

"Fair enough," Angela said as she withdrew her hand. "Gormanski said you could help us figure out a device."

"Yes, yes," The Historian said as he gestured for Angela and Octan to follow him through a door that lead into a structure under the bridge. "Welcome to the temple of broken toys."

Inside was a massive warehouse were dozens of people, mostly those looking just as wayward as the Historian. They all were all working together in a large collective.

"What is this place?" Octan asked, looking around as the people inside tinkered with all manner of technology, most of which far obsolete and little looking like it went with the others.

"This is a place where we hang onto the value of that which people think has no value," The Historian said, leading them though to a makeshift office at the end. "We live in a society with an industry based within the law of diminished returns. You make a better mousetrap and you make a fortune … but you will make less and less of a fortune unless you keep making a better and better mousetrap.

"People will tend to stop buying technology if they are not excited by it," Octan agreed. "And to keep it exciting is the real challenge."

"Quoted well from a Wikipedia article," The Historian said as he sat down at a desk. "You are right, however. The computer technological revolution made diamonds from sand. The idea of a computer was not known to many even a hundred years ago, but then BAM … seemingly overnight a new world came out. This seemed alien to most but the promise began. Computers and technology can change your life. Look at this thing, it can do this thing … and look out, maybe soon, it will do twice as much. People bought into the idea of the computer evolving dream more than the computer themselves. It was like a god rush, but instead of gold it was silicon and bytes."

"You preserve the idea of what computers are?" Angela speculated. "Not by what they could be?"

"Exactly!" The Historian said in an encouraged tone. "There is beauty in the machines and a certain wisdom in some of the connections. You see for every Darpanet or Apple, there are an equal number of things that did not lead to more. These ideas are not wrong in themselves, they are just not the ones that chance shows as the winner."

"Like laserdisc and beta," Octan added. "Perfectly decent technologies that just did not happen to become en-vouge."

"One as young as you knows what laserdisc is?" The Historian commented. "I am impressed."

"I like to read," Octan commented. "Technology fascinates me, even the stuff before my time."

"Good, good," The Historian commented. "Show me what you have."

Octan nodded and took the transport device out of its bag. "It is mostly untouched from the … people we got it from. I just added an external power source so it's battery didn't die."

"Good job you did of it too," The Historian said as he looked over the device. "This is a solid-state device."

"Solid state?" Angela asked.

"Most data storage devices rely on electromagnetic storage." Octan explained. "Like a SD card or a hard drive. Solid state charges something with electrons and therefore does not rely on as complicated an apparatus."

"I want to headhunt this kid," The Historian said with a grin. "Yes, this is solid state technology. Very popular in the fifties and sixties and mostly forgotten when magnetic tape became popular. Though I think it is due for a comeback. Would you believe there was a conspiracy to suppress this kind of technology?"

"You would be surprised how much we believe that," Angela added. "We have seen some serious stuff."

"The components in this device were from several companies that literally disappeared off the face of the earth," The Historian continued. "This device and ones like it could reputedly hold terabytes of information when the next closest devices could hold bytes … like less than fifty. However, just as it seemed poised to take over it was gone."

"Well, we suspect the people that we got this from suppressed it," Angela replied. "But that is a different story entirely."

"Can you read it?" Octan asked. "Be careful with what is on it … it's irreplaceable data."

"Old technology or new technology," The Historian replied as he Frankensteined some cables together. "Important data is important data."

A computer screen lit up next to him, showing massive amounts of data scrolling almost too fast to read."

"You must understand we cannot tell you what this is," Angela replied. "But it is of the utmost importance we figure it out."

"You don't need to," The Historian said as he stared at the screen, his eyes fixed to it like he was Moses receiving the Ten Commandments. "I can tell what this is … it is life."

"How could you possibly know?" Octan asked. "It is gibberish to me and I am probably one of the best coders in this seaboard."

"It is beyond a program," The Historian replied. "It is a living, thinking thing. Programmers have been trying to make a system of artificial intelligence for years … but this … this was what gave them the dream."

"You have seen it before?" Angela asked. "Data like this."

"I was not much older than you," The Historian said as he gestured to Octan. "I was a vonderkind and working for a small company named Nadest Investments. We were doing all sorts of stuff, networking computers before people knew what a network could do. A guy came in, he had a device unlike anything we had ever seen before."

Angela nodded. She knew it had to be Hurst, way back as he was trying to gain a foothold on this world.

"It is a consciousness," Angela replied, realizing there was no point in beating around the bush. "It is not from this world and it wants very much for us … to become like it."

"You don't need to tell me the dangers of that," The Historian replied. "I am friends with Gormanski after all."

"True enough," Angela agreed. "We need your help and we need it rather quickly."

"Anything," The Historian offered. "Name it."

"We need to know how to kill it," Angela replied. "Not just for the one in there, but how to kill them all."

The historian laughed. "That should not be a problem. If there is one thing we know all too well here … that's how to break things!"

***

The resources provided by The Historian and his people had proven to be the greatest benefit since Hurst had given them all of the answers from before. They had a theoretical solution and a way to hurt the aliens and this filled Angela with some much-needed hope. The Historian gave them all the tech they would need to access the device, others like it, and to do what needed to be done. His only stipulation was that they not test it in his facility. This suited Angela just fine as she preferred to do it with Hina and Gormanski present so they might offer insights into the process.

Not long after, Angela and Octan returned to the cabin to discuss things with the others and plan for what was to come next.

"I trust that the trip was successful?" Gormanski asked as the pair came into the cabin and began to set up the gear.

"Incredibly so," Angela replied with an encouraging tone. "Your … Historian was quite a character."

"I would say they don't make many men like him anymore," Gormanski commented. "But there were never many quite like that guy."

"Well he managed to not only get us access but explain how we can hurt them," Angela replied.

"Hurt them?" Octan added. "We can kill them."

"Please explain," Gormanski asked as Octan set up the equipment.

"Well, the best way to put it is like the gravitational co-ordinates, each alien has a distinct pattern," Angela explained. "A massively large wavelength of information that basically forms out their brain."

"Our brains are very similar … hence why they can overwrite us," Octan jumped in. "However, we know very little about how our brains work, only that electrons fire in a sequence to make up our intelligence, motor controls, and most importantly our consciousness. The aliens seem to have found a way to remove the entire process and simulate it in a free form that does not degrade or mix with other."

"Each alien is different," Angela continued. "Like a fingerprint or a snowflake, their consciousness's enter a state of kind of suspended animation. When they are like this, they are not conscious but kind of on hold, waiting for a new host to start up again."

"So, that guy in the machine is not aware that something is wrong?" Hina asked as she watched Octan set the machine up to The Historians tech.

"It is like they are asleep," Octan commented. "They do not risk degradation, and to do this they needed to compress everything onto kind of a transportable state. Last thing this guy likely remembers is being whatever the hell they were before and sending himself into the machine."

"And presumably they are lining up and preparing to send millions of them," Gormanski added. "If they have not started already."

"Well, this is how they are venerable," Angela added. "In this frozen state, we can destroy them."

"And how do we do that?" Gormanski added. "Did you find a way to unravel them, to corrupt or destroy the data?"

"Not exactly," Octan replied. "They are easy enough to destroy. If I took the power source out of this machine the data would degrade and fall apart. It is simple enough to destroy one … we needed to find a way to destroy them all."

"Then how do we do that?" Gormanski added. "Like a cascading virus?"

"No," Angela replied. "Each of these aliens is a system of equations that is far more advanced than even the entirety of The Historian's crew and we could decode in a lifetime. However, we were able to decipher some commands from the device, including one that will really help us. You see when this thing is hooked up to a person it makes a connection though their cerebral cortex and it sends the alien consciousness one command."

"Decompress," Octan replied with a smile. "It says to it there is a vessel here, decompress and take it over."

"But what happens if there is no vessel?" Gormanski asked.

"They decompress into nothingness," Angela replied. "Imagine you wanted to toss several papers across the room to Hina. Your best bet is to fold them into a small strong parcel and toss them. However, should it open up in flight it would spray the papers all over the ground. The device is crude at best and all of our technology on this side is the same. Once the decompression command is given there is no failsafe, no turning back. If the alien does not have a place to go his data hemorrhages out and is irretrievable."

"So, you want to put that command into the storage device?" Gormanski asked. "Tell them to spontaneously decompress like they are ready. But how do we get them all?"

"That is the beauty of it," Octan said with a smile. "They are literally rigged to do nothing except decompress and there is a command for doing it on a bigger scale. It basically says decompress, then pass to X number after you to decompress as well. X in this case meaning how many hosts in total are standing by."

"So, if you said decompress and signal 5 it would decompress and tell the next alien decompress and signal 4?" Hina asked.

"Exactly," Angela replied. "This is a way to theoretically set up several hosts at a time and load them quickly with several aliens."

"What if we said decompress and signal infinite?" Gormanski said, his eyes wide. "Would it decompress then keep telling the next and the next forever?"

Angela nodded. "It would be completely unstoppable until it ran out of consciousness' to link to. In theory, it could even go back though the link and decompress any that were compressed on their home network."

"A simple yet elegant solution," Gormanski replied. "I can't believe it is so simple."

"To be honest, it is the alien's assumption that we cannot access their technology that is working for us," Angela explained. "Combined with the destruction of their plan B facility it means all their eggs are in one basket."

"They know if they make the invasion too slow it might fail," Hina added. "Like if they do not have enough hosts people might get wise and make like a resistance."

"Exactly!" Angela replied. "Their best bet it to get the bulk of their minds here so they can flood the world before we can get wise to it."

"Do we have any way to test it?" Gormanski asked. "Can we be sure the command will do as anticipated."

"Well, we only have the one alien to test with," Octan replied. "But The Historian made a simulation of the alien order that will make this one think the sequence before it had decompressed and spread the exponent. I have it set now. All I have to do is set the number to simulate and once it reaches zero it will execute the command to the living alien."

"Set it to three," Hina suggested. "It is my favorite number."

Octan nodded, setting it for three. "Who wants the honors?"

"All we got to do is press the button and we end a life?" Gormanski replied. "Literally the biggest fear of the technological revolution."

"You would flinch now?" Angela asked.

"Of course, not," Gormanski said with a nod. "I killed one of those sons of bitches' face to face. I have no issue pressing a button to do it … I just wanted to state the significance of the setup."

"I would like to do it," Angela said. "I have never killed anything before … intentionally at least. I am going to Antarctica and if I will hesitate I want to know now."

"Be my guest," Gormanski replied. "You have seen more of their evil than any of us. I cannot imagine you would hesitate."

"No," Angela said as she pressed the button immediately. "I am long done hesitating."

The simulation began … decompressing, signal 2 … decompressing signal 1, decompressing, signal 0. The device lit up, a whining sound beginning and the lights lighting up before going blank and shitting the machine off.

"It worked!" Octan replied. "There is no data on the machine. The pattern wavelength decompressed and corrupted into nothing."

"We have it!" Gormanski replied. "The sword of Damocles … waiting to smite down the wicked with the righteous hand of god."

Everyone looked to Gormanski with looks of confused curiosity on their faces.

"I'm excited, ok?" Gormanski commented. "I have never had the power to destroy an entire evil alien organization before."

"So, what is our next step?" Octan asked. "How do we execute this plan and give the signal to the rest of them?"

"Well it is both easy and very hard," Angela replied. "The easy part … in nothing other than comparison is that we need to get a couple of us to Antarctica. Second and the more challenging one is that we need a device that somehow will get us past security and seem like a normal piece of tech, but be powerful enough to override any and all failsafes once we get to the base."

"I should be the one that goes with you," Hina replied. "I know NASA systems better than anyone here and I will be able to easier adapt to any roadblocks we might find."

"Agreed," Angela replied. "But don't the rest of you worry, we have a lot to do as well."

"Well we will all work together to build the device," Octan replied. "But, after you go, what did you have in mind?"

"Well, we have a bit of advantage that they do not know we are coming," Angela replied. "At best, they do not know we have betrayed NASA. At worse we need to fall back onto fake personas."

"I can be ready for either," Hina replied "I just need a little time."

"Though we could use all the help we could get to make it so while they should be looking for us to come they are otherwise distracted," Angela suggested. "Their attention locked elsewhere."

"Perhaps it is time to blow this thing wide open," Gormanski replied. "Leak the information to the press, the net and to the public at large."

"What part of the information?" Octan asked.

"All of it," Gormanski replied proudly. "We literally dump the unedited information of EVERYRHING NASA is doing or has done and let everyone sort it out."

"NASA will of course try to discredit all of it," Angela replied. "Try to get it lost in the chafe."

"Well, this is the final battle, right?" Gormanski added. "Balls to the wall. NASA knows I am a past threat ... I'd prove to show them they should not have taken me off the radar."

"I can blast us worldwide and it would take them weeks to silence us," Octan replied. "Like pirate radio."

"Exactly!" Gormanski shouted. "We ring the bells and call out to the heavens and see who listens."

"I like it," Angela agreed. "Even if is only serves to piss NASA off and make them think that your broadcast is the real threat."

"They will forget about anything else!" Gormanski said with a grin. "This has been a long time coming and I am going to enjoy each and every second of it!"

"Then it is settled," Angela replied. "According to our best guesses, they will have the capability to receive within a few days. We then give them a week to amass as much of the aliens as they can. We spend four days on the device and prep and take the rest of the time to get Hina and I to Antarctica. This is going to take all of our skillsets and more than a little luck but we are humanities best hope."

"Sounds like a movie," Octan said with a grin. "We are like heroes."

"Not yet," Angela said with a smile. "Right now, we are just the best chances of victory. Let us wait to see if we are successful or not to see how we are regarded. We are only heroes if we win."

***

Hina had spent a long time making perfect new identifies for herself and Angela. This was something that normally should not have been quite so easy, but Hina did still have a lot of resources from NASA, as well as a set of skills that only were shared by a only a handful of people in the entire world. It was very effective and soon enough they were on a plane and found themselves in Port Stanley in the Balkan islands.

It was not airstrips that NASA was primarily buying out it was shipping lines. This was the largest and most efficient ways to get people to and from Antarctica and mostly based on boats and commercial cruise ships. The ports were filled with people as NASA seemed to be gathering people en-mass through fake contests, military maneuvering and every trick up their sleeve. They were not moving people yet. They were likely still gathering, but this meant that Angela and Hina did not have much time.

The pair found that there was a private yacht moving VIPS to the site that was leaving that day. It took Hina exactly twenty minutes to fabricate a digital id for both of them to make it look like they were both high ranking members of the Turkish government. Soon they were on the yacht and on their way. It would be a few days trip, even on the speedy craft and they needed every moment to prepare.

The device that they would use was a simple laptop. It was professed by Octan and Hina to be one of the most expensive and powerful laptops in the world, though they went to great lengths to make it not look the part. They put it in the shell of a cheap bargain brand laptop and aged it to look like it had been through some things and was refurbished. It looked like a run of the mill travel laptop and something that would never arise suspicion. The NASA security people could even scan it … there was a fake dummy drive that simulated a simple operating system and shielding the hidden real drive. Hina boasted that when the computer was truly unleashed, none of NASA's security measures were likely to be able to stand up to it.

Octan and Hina had worked tirelessly on the device while Gormanski and Angela mostly made preparations. Though they had only parted ways a few days before Angela felt melancholy, missing her friends already. Though they had come together mostly by necessity and to fight a greater evil, she realized she enjoyed it greatly. She admitted that she usually left little time for friends in her life … at least not meaningful relationships and was glad to have these people around. She formed strong bonds with them and her greatest hope was that after it all was over, after everything was settled that she could continue to see these people who were now an integral part of her life. She put this idea on the back burner for now as there was still much work to be done and it would not help to get lost in it for the time being.

The hot and warm temperature of the south began to turn cold and by the time they reached the Antarctic seas, it was colder than Angela had been in a long time. They had, of course, packed for this eventuality but it was still very cold. This would work to their advantage to an effect. Though Hina and Angela both cut and died their hair they knew there was a possibility they would be recognized. The cold weather gear and layers would help them pass unnoticed.

Normally Antarctica was only traversable by a small few and it was challenging. But as they reached the Antarctic they discovered that it was filled with an unprecedented amount of activity. Aircraft carriers, special craft and brand new structures filled the area. It was not long until the yacht was docked and they were being brought to what looked like a tunnel into the ice. Soldiers arrived to look over who had come. Luckily, having chosen VIP's, they were treated well and Hina's hastily generated identification passed initial inspection with flying colors.

Inside the tunnel was a makeshift steel bunker and within that was a rail system. They were told that it was miles to the site and this was the best way to make it. Angela got on a train with Hina and soon it got underway. The train was only half filled but seemed to be one of many they shipped down to Antarctica to prepare for a massive number of people to come. This was it. There was no turning back and Angela took Hina to one of the empty compartments to go over some things.

"How are you feeling?" Angela asked, closing the door and sweeping for bugs with a device before she began.

"Everything seems ready to go," Hina replied. "Everything's charged and I have a secure link to headquarters."

"That is not what I meant," Angela replied. "I mean how are you feeling … inside? You doing ok?"

"Oh, I am nervous for sure," Hina replied. "But I am confident that I will function as well as the computer."

"Good," Angela said with a nod. "I know this isn't exactly a situation you can truly be ready for."

"You always seem to be," Hina commented with a smile. "No matter what they throw at you, I see you adapt to it."

"Say what you will about NASA's behind the scenes …" Angela commented. "But they do train their astronauts well. On the surface, the dream is very powerful and the training to actually achieve those dreams is nothing short of remarkable. We are taught to expect the unexpected and to go with whatever occurs."

"Well, you are like my hero," Hina commented. "I just want you to know that."

Angela smiled. "That means a lot to me. There are a lot of people, good people that I cared about in NASA that I had to leave behind. I am glad you came with me … to do what had to be done."

"I tend to drift in life," Hina admitted. "My parents planned out my life when I was a kid. They told me what I was to become … even who I was to marry. I always avoided it. I had my own dreams my own desires. I suppose I lived a selfish existence and did not care."

"Following your dreams is not selfish," Angela replied. "It is the responsibility of a true dreamer."

Hina smiled. "I got disowned for my dreams and I told myself that I did it for the right reasons … it was not until I started working with you that I actually felt like I did the right thing. This whole mess … I feel like we are supposed to be doing it."

"I think so too," Angela replied. "We have come way too far to flinch now."

"We should go over everything again," Hina said with a smile. "We should check and doublecheck it one last time."

Angela nodded. "Let's do it. We can't ensure we will have much luck, but we can make damn sure that we are prepared."

The pair went through all of their equipment and made sure that it was all primed, working and ready to go. Within an hour, a squealing of brakes could be heard and the train slowed to a stop. Ahead was a massive stone building with likely the largest satellite disk on earth behind it. Only the massive money embezzled from countless countries could have built something like this in Antarctica. It stood as a monument of corruption and a stark reminded of the power that was being wielded against them.

As they arrived at the base, things seemed very busy. NASA was, no doubt, using much of their personnel to deal with the oncoming flood of hosts that they were spread pretty thin. Nonetheless they were rescanning ID's even for the VIPS and going through extensive checks.

"Will our new backgrounds hold up to this?" Angela asked. "This seems like the most ridged screening that we are likely to see."

"I hope so," Hina replied. "Then again, I have never been this high in clearance before."

Angela touched a hand to her earpiece. "Any chance you can begin the broadcast?"

"Born ready," she heard Gormanski reply eagerly. "Here goes."

Angela could hear Gormanski clear his throat, readying for a broadcast that was about to go everywhere.

"I speak now to all of those who seek the truth and know that they are being deceived," Gormanski began. "I will not beat around the bush. NASA has been lying to you and I am here to share with you everything … every bit of it."

Angela listened to Gormanski lay out the background of the aliens plans in impressive detail as the line moved. Each person going through a thorough screening and moving on. Hina and Angela got to the front and their ID's were scanned. The guard went to do some searches when he paused, putting his finger to his headpiece.

"Hey there seems to be some sort of problem in HQ," the guard said as he looked up. "They are recalling us to help deal with some PR problem."

"Well that happens to be my specialty," Hina jumped in. "If we can hurry this up I can set up my laptop and get them to shut down anything NASA needs."

The guard looked up at Hina, his hands still hovering over the keyboard to his computer. "Yeah ... go ahead."

The guard handed back Hina and Angela their ID's and waved them through. Hina smiled and moved on as the guard closed his station and conversed with the other guard.

"Thank you Gormanski," Angela said to herself as she listened to him linking to multiple evidence they had collected and where people could freely view it.

As the broadcast went on, the base became more erratic. NASA was under attack from the net and they reacted as if they were under attack in real life. They seemed to think this was a precursor to some sort of larger event and began to close down the base. Luckily, for Angela and Hina who were already inside, this meant they were right where they wanted to be. The pair paused next to a floor map to figure out their next move.

"They do not list where the server is," Angela replied. "It would be silly for them to have it on the map I guess."

"Show it to Octan," Hina replied. "He has like a sixth sense to design."

Angela nodded, holding up her secured personal phone and taking a picture of the map. Within seconds Gormanski's voice dimmed in her headpiece and Octan came on.

"The central area known as the arboretum," Octan commented. "It is a direct line from satellite control and there is no way that NASA gives two craps about plants up there."

"Good!" Angela commented as she directed Hina to follow her. "How are things going on that end?"

"Gormanski is having the time of his life," Octan commented. "I am tracking them trying to find us. I have made so many rabbit holes for them to check it will take them weeks to explore them all."

"Be careful," Angela commented. "If they get too close, log off and go silent."

"You're in a supervillain layer in Antarctica," Octan commented. "You are the ones who should be careful."

"We all should," Angel commented. "Talk to you soon."

Octan went back to work and Gormanski continued talking as Hina and Angela snuck past patrols and made their way deeper and deeper into the compound.

"NASA was created to better mankind and we believed it," Gormanski went on. "But it was slowly, little by little taken over by the very thing they wanted to share with humanity … the unknown. These travelers of the stars might seem unbelievable but they are here, there has been signs of it for years. NASA has hidden it like they hid everything else and punished those who spoke up and asked questions."

Eventually Hina and Angela reached a massive security door that was labeled as the arboretum. There was a complex security lock and Angela looked to Hina. She nodded, taking out some tech and going to work on the door. She was not at it for a minute when a guard came by and stopped to look at the pair.

"What are you doing here?" The guard demanded. "This whole site is on lockdown!"

"We were sent here by Enrick," Angela said in her best lie. "We are top level analyst's."

"I was told to let no one come to this level," the guard replied. "By Enrick himself."

"Well, I can show you the text he himself sent me," Angela replied. "May I approach."

"Yes," the guard replied. "Let's see it."

Angela took out her phone and approached the guard. As she held up her phone for him to see she switched hands and then savagely slammed her elbow into his throat as hard as she could. The guard staggered back, clutching his throat and struggling to breathe. Angela then picked up a fire extinguisher and smashed him over the head, knocking him out cold.

"Shit!" Hina said out loud. "That was amazing."

Angela smiled back though she felt guilty for what she had done. She grabbed the guard and dragged him out of sight before returning. "How are we doing with the door?"

Hina smiled as the door beeped and slowly opened. Inside was a massive chamber that, as Octan suggested, held absolutely no plants. Instead was a titanic sized neuro computer that literally composed the inside of the dome like room, all culminating in a central pillar on a raised platform going into the heart of the room. Hina and Angela rushed across the room and went to a terminal to start their work. Hina set up the advanced laptop and began to get out cables.

"Start patching me in just like we practiced," Hina replied. "This computer is likely like simulation three."

Angela nodded, having taken a crash course in many of the world's most advanced supercomputers in preparation for the mission. It was challenging, but soon she had the laptop hooked in. Hina booted up the computer and went to work. Angela kept watch but admitted that there seemed to be a lot of side entrances into this room and she did not know what she would do if she were caught. She had taken a sidearm from the incapacitated guard and tucked it into the back of her pants. She knew that she would make herself do whatever was necessary but really did not want to use any more lethal force than she needed to.

"I have never seen anything like this," Hina admitted. "We were not prepared for this."

"What's wrong," Angela said, coming over to Hina on the computer and looking over her shoulder. "Can we not get to the alien storage modules?"

"I can't even log in," Hina admitted. "This is a level of security beyond anything I have seen before."

"Can you crack it?" Angela asked. "Can you force our way in?"

"I can force it for sure," Hina admitted. "But the computer is on lockdown and secured. If I force our way in, the computer will set off alarms and manually cut power to this terminal. I have to sneak in and it will not be easy."

"But can you do it?" Angela asked.

"Yeah," Hina agreed. "But it will take some time."

"Ok you do that," Angela replied. "I think I might have a backup idea. I have …"

The unmistakable sound of a gunshot rang through the massive chamber. Hina looked down at herself and blood began to flow out from the exit wound on her shoulder. She instinctively grabbed it and slumped into the chair. Angela drew her gun from her belt and turned around to see Enrick standing several feet behind with his gun out."

"Drop it!" Enrick shouted. "I will shoot you both dead. You know I will."

Angela dropped her gun and glared at Enrick. "I suppose I would have been disappointed if we did not see each other face to face by the end."

"End for you perhaps," Enrick replied. "We are just at the beginning … a new beginning."

"Not if we can help it," Angela retorted as Enrick drew closer.

"I am so very upset to see that it was indeed you that has betrayed us," Enrick explained. "Stone had such high praise of you and we dared not think you had betrayed him."

"I would do it again," Angela replied proudly. "You have no idea the things I would to protect this world."

"I will give you that," Enrick replied. "Protecting one's people is the responsibility of all. I am doing the same."

"So, are you going to kill us?" Angela asked. "If so, get on with it."

"Oh, I will kill you both eventually," Enrick replied. "But I need you to tell me where your friend is broadcasting from."

Angela nodded, that was why he shot Hina and not her, and why the wound was potentially non-fatal. Angela smiled. "You can't silence him, can you? That must really stick in your craw doesn't it?"

"You will tell me how to shut them down," Enrick insisted. "Like you, I will do anything for the protection of my people. We are no different."

"You cannot suggest that this is fine what you have done," Angela replied. "Protecting your people is one thing … but to kill so many to do it is something else entirely."

"It is a resource we must take," Enrick replied. "It is as simple as that."

"Fine," Angela replied. "I will show you how to track the transmission."

"Good!" Enrick replied. "Tell me now!"

Angela slowly reached into her jacket, withdrawing a pair of cellphones, holding one in each hand. She then stared at Enrick with pure hatred on his face.

"What is this?" Enrick asked. "What is the function of those phones?"

"This one is off and dead," Angela said, holding up the one in her right hand slightly. "This is a phone that belonged to another astronaut, a woman very much like me who just wanted to grow plants in space. You had her murdered and it was what showed me what I was fighting against … no matter how noble you profess your intentions to be."

"Such inconsequential nonsense," Enrick replied. "We do not have ties for wasted sentiment. What is the other?"

"This?" Angela said as she held up the phone in her left hand and touched the screen and opened an application. "This is Stone's phone … it seems it's already connected to this network and I just linked it to our computer in front of Hina."

"No!" Enrick shouted as he looked over to Hina. Even in shock, even while bleeding, she took a second to smile before quickly reaching forward and executing the code. The command was away and nothing could stop it now.

Enrick ran forward, running to a terminal and trying to pull it up to stop it. However, as he went to work he started shouting in frustration. "What did you do?"

"We blew your minds," Angela said with a smile. "All of them."

"They are decompressing!" Enrick shouted. "The whole network!"

Angela watched as the computer displayed the minds in the system come apart one by one. Enrick struggled to shut down the uplink but before he was even half way to doing it the decompression order was in the stream and was out of his hands. Within another minute the machine went silent … no sign of alien life in it at all.

"Do you know what you have done?" Enrick said, thronging to ward Angela. "You potentially have caused genocide!"

"Beat you to it I guess," Angela replied. "Got your people before you got mine."

"Do you expect that you are going to walk out of here?" Enrick said, pointing his gun at Angela. "I should shoot you dead on the spot for what you just did."

"We did have one contingency plan in effect," Angela admitted. "The world now knows EVERYTHING you did. However, there is one thing we did not tell them."

"And what is that?" Enrick asked.

"Well, there's no more of you coming," Angel replied. "Though there are a fair amount of you still here. Soon there will be a lot of nations demanding answers and uncovering the corruption. There will be a witch-hunt where they will try to search out every alien."

"What of it?" Enrick asked, seeming to be unable to debate what might be coming.

"Well, we know a way to detect which of you are aliens," Angela replied with a smile. "A rather simple device that is accessible to almost anyone and I tested it out on you in fact."

"This is not out there?" Enrick asked, seeming to show something on his face that encouraged Angela … it was fear.

"Not yet," Angela replied. "Though I have set it up that if ANYTHING happens to me or my crew it gets automatically sent. Imagine how much people will want to see it should it go out."

Enrick sighed and lowered his gun. "I accept your terms."

"We will be leaving now," Angela said as she went to Hina and started to perform first aid to stop the bleeding. "We will require use of a med bay and a doctor, then we will be on our way."

"Fine," Enrick commented as he fell to his knees. "Take anything you like … you have already won."

Angela patched up Hina the best she could and began to help her out of the chamber. As they got to the door another gunshot rang through the hall. Angela looked back to see the body of Enrick slide to the floor, seemingly he could not live with his failure and joined his people in oblivion.

"Did we do it?" Hina asked weekly as she walked with Angela. "Did we win?"

"We did," Angela said as she smiled to Hina. "We won."

***

Two weeks later Angela was back at the cabin with the others. Hina had made a full recovery, but would require much physical rehabilitation to fully regain use of her shoulder. Octan and Gormanski were like celebrities now, heralded as the ones who blew the corruption of NASA wide open. There was a private celebration for the group and what they had accomplished. It would be some time before the world knew everything of what happened but that was fine. The world at large had a lot to come to terms with and it would take time for them to reconcile all of it. During the party a black car pulled up into the driveway and just sat there … Idling.

"Should we be worried?" Octan asked to Angela.

"No," Angela replied. "This is just one last loose end to tie up. I will be right back."

Angela walked out as Hurst got out of the car. Within another figure sat, waiting for Hurst to return.

"You did well," Hurst replied. "Even I was surprised by your tactics."

"We may not be star travelers but humans are nothing if not resourceful," Angela replied.

"Well you did your job well," Hurst admitted. "Every one of us not in human form is gone and what you did went back, probably all the way to our current home world. They shut off all communications from that end. They seemed to have gotten hit hard and have quarantined themselves from this world."

"Will there be reprisals?" Angela asked. "Another attempt."

"My people are paranoid," Hurst replied. "We got hurt hard and the last thing they will want to do is risk any more. I cannot say if they will try to find somewhere else or not but you can be sure this is the last place they will ever come again."

"That is encouraging," Angela replied. "So, what about you?"

"I will keep my promise as you have kept yours," Hurst replied. "My partner and I are officially retired and after this meeting you will never hear of us again."

"That is what we arranged," Angela nodded. "Thank you for everything."

"No need for thanks," Hurst replied as he looked around the area. "It is beautiful here."

"It is," Angela relied. "With everything that happened I forgot to notice things like this. Now that the earth is safe it feels brand new, so vibrant and splendid."

"That makes sense," Hurst nodded. "So, what about you? What will you do now?"

"No clue," Angela replied. "I'm an ex-astronaut that hasn't thought much about what life holds for her, other than space. I don't even know what will happen with NASA."

"It is still there," Hurst replied as he moved back to his car and opened the door. "There is still a need for it and good people there that remain. It is hurting now but can be repaired with the right moves and the right person."

"I suppose that is up to the new director of NASA, isn't it?" Angela asked.

"That it is," Hurst replied. "You have a lot of work ahead of you Director McGee."

With that Hurst closed the door and drove off, leaving Angela behind to decide for herself what was next for a humanity and earth now back in the hands of the people where it belongs.

END